P9-CZV-829

More praise for
SPYING ON MISS MÜLLER

"The use of telling details defines the girls
and the faculty members so that the fast-
moving plot has an inevitability that rings
true."
—*School Library Journal*

"Highly readable . . . More than a spy story."
—*Booklist* (starred review)

By Eve Bunting
Published by Fawcett Books:

A SUDDEN SILENCE
SPYING ON MISS MÜLLER

SPYING ON MISS MÜLLER

Eve Bunting

FAWCETT JUNIPER • NEW YORK

"We're Gonna Hang Out the Wash on the Siegfried Line"
Words and music by Jimmy Kennedy and Michael Carr
Copyright © 1939 by Skidmore Music Co., Inc.
Copyright renewed   International copyright secured
All rights reserved

A Fawcett Juniper Book
Published by Ballantine Books
Copyright © 1995 by Eve Bunting

http://www.randomhouse.com

Library of Congress Catalog Card Number: 96-96463

ISBN 0-449-70455-6

Manufactured in the United States of America

First Edition: November 1996

10 9 8 7 6 5 4 3 2 1

*For my friends, Janet and Jim, who
encouraged me, and for my "Alveara" friends.
They know who they are.*

1

"CAN YOU REMEMBER how much we used to like Miss Müller?" Maureen asked the rest of us.

"Well, we don't like her anymore," Ada said.

The four of us—Maureen, Ada, Lizzie Mag, and I—were sprawled on my bed just before lights-out. We were wearing our blue regulation pajamas and dressing gowns and I had my blue quilt wrapped around me. The dorm was always freezing.

"She *does* look like Vivien Leigh, though," I said. We'd seen *Gone With the Wind* at the Imperial Cinema last Saturday, and we were boggled by Vivien Leigh as Scarlett O'Hara.

"Miss Müller's sweeter looking," Lizzie Mag said.

"Don't say sweet about a German," Ada told her sharply. "Germans are poison."

Miss Müller taught German and she'd been everybody's favorite teacher until Britain went to war with Germany. Northern Ireland is part of Britain, so it was our war, too. Most of the boarders at the Alveara school had fathers, brothers, uncles serving in the army or the navy or the Royal Air Force. My favorite cousin, Bryan, was in the army fighting Germans somewhere in France.

1

Bryan was like a brother to me, since I didn't have a brother, or a sister either. Now he was in danger, and here we were with Miss Müller, a half German, the dorm mistress in our dormitory.

"We're contaminated," Ada Sinclair said.

Secretly I didn't think we were contaminated. I still liked Miss Müller. But I was careful not to defend her too much. It was awful to be called Jessie the German lover, and that's what Mean Jean Ross had called me at break last Friday. In front of two of the boy boarders, too.

I was trying not to defend Miss Müller now.

"She could be a spy for all we know," Maureen Campbell said.

"Like Mata Hari," Ada added. Ada read, so she knew a lot.

Maureen dropped her knitting onto the bed between her bent knees. She'd been knitting a balaclava helmet for months, the kind that comes right over one's face and leaves only slits for eyes. When it was finished she'd send it to one of the boys at the front along with a very flattering photograph of herself that she'd taken in the booth at Woolworth's, a front view and two profiles for a shilling. Maureen looked seventeen instead of thirteen. The rest of us just looked thirteen.

Maureen had suggested she send the helmet and the photograph to my cousin Bryan.

"He might like to be my pen pal," she'd said.

"Forget it, Mo," I told her. "Keep your mitts off him." Maureen was such a shark where boys were concerned. She picked up her knitting again now and frowned at it.

I'd been home for the weekend and had brought back a

bar of Cadbury's fruit-and-nut chocolate. We finished off the last four squares.

"But what kind of spying could Miss Müller do at Alveara?" Lizzie Mag licked chocolate off her fingers and went back to the subject of our conversation.

"She'd be spying from here, using us as camouflage. Reporting back to Hitler," Maureen said.

"On one of those Morse code radios, you mean?" Lizzie Mag asked.

"Dit-da-dit, dit-da-dit, attention all ships at sea." Ada crossed her eyes.

"And where would she keep this dit-da-dit machine?" I asked as sarcastically as I could.

"Somewhere in her room," Ada said promptly.

"We could look," Maureen suggested.

We stared at one another.

"Oh, we'd be in terrible trouble if we got caught," Lizzie Mag said. "Being in a teacher's room without permission. Poking through her things."

Maureen raised her eyebrows. They used to be thick and black, but she shaved them off and now used a soft 2B pencil to draw in arched lines. "The Arcs de Triomphe" Ada called them, after the famous arch in Paris. "She's not a teacher anymore," Maureen said. "She's a German."

"If the Secret Service or the police were suspicious of Miss Müller, they'd have sent her away to one of those camps in England," I said.

"They only take men," Maureen said authoritatively. "And no one would ever think Miss Müller was a man."

We shook our heads, all of us visualizing Miss Müller's cute, slim figure with the movie-star breasts. Hers were

3

real, too; we could tell by the way they wobbled. They weren't just handkerchiefs stuffed into a bra. Maureen did that all the time and it was so obvious.

"Girls."

"Oh, cheese," Maureen groaned. "Here comes the Fräulein and I just dropped a stitch."

"Time for bed check," Miss Müller called in her soft voice with the little accent that we used to think so attractive. For a while we'd even practiced talking with accents ourselves.

We'd loved her name, too. Daphne.

"Like a beautiful daffodil," Lizzie Mag had said.

"Daphne was a nymph," Ada told her. "Apollo was in love with her. She was changed into a laurel tree."

"I'd rather be a daffodil," Maureen had said.

We used to think we were lucky having Miss Müller be the teacher in our dorm. Not anymore.

"Lights out in five minutes," Miss Müller said. "Please make sure you have all your things ready in case of an air raid."

"Let's check her room tonight, right after lights-out," Ada whispered. "Soon as she leaves to go to the teachers' lounge."

"I'm not going to," I said. "It's too sneaky."

"You're her little pet, that's why you're not going." Maureen pushed her face close to mine. I could smell the chocolate on her breath. I was wishing I hadn't shared. "You don't have to come," she said. "The rest of us will carry out the inspection." She gathered her knitting and left. Over her shoulder she said, "It's our duty. It's for the war effort."

Lizzie Mag, whose cubicle is next to mine, didn't

4

leave with the other two. Her face shone with cold cream and her blond hair was pinned up in little tight curls. I never wore cold cream at night because it encourages pimples, and mine didn't need encouraging. I never put my frizzy red hair in pin curls either. What would have been the use?

"Do you think Ada and Maureen will really do it?" Lizzie Mag whispered.

I rolled my eyes. "Probably," I said. "They're daft enough for anything."

"Thanks for sharing the chocolate," Lizzie Mag said.

"I got it with my daddy's sweetie coupons. He saved them for me. They were the last ones in his ration book." Suddenly I saw him giving them to me. His smile, the love in his eyes. My throat tightened.

"He's so nice, Jessie. And so handsome, too," Lizzie Mag said. "Just like a film star. Is he any better?"

"A bit." I bent and took off my slippers so I wouldn't have to look at her. I dreaded being asked about my father.

Lizzie Mag gave me a quick hug. "Night, Jess."

As she left my cubicle, she called "Good night" to everyone in Snow White.

Snow White was the name of our dorm. We hated it that all the dorms had fairy-tale names. It was so babyish for fourth formers.

Already I could hear Miss Müller opening the door of the first cubie, which was Maureen's. "Good night, dear. How does the knitting progress?"

"Very well, thank you, Miss Müller."

You'd think butter wouldn't melt in Maureen's mouth,

and here she was planning to search Miss Müller's room that very night.

"Good night, Ada. What are you reading?"

"It's *All Quiet on the Western Front*, Miss Müller. It's about the First World War, when we fought the Germans the last time."

I held my breath. That Ada. She didn't care what she said.

"Yes. I have read the novel myself," Miss Müller said. "We must discuss it when you've finished."

She opened Lizzie Mag's door. "Good night, Elizabeth Margaret."

Lizzie Mag was named after the two English princesses, Elizabeth and Margaret. But only the teachers ever called her that. Lizzie Mag's parents lived in India. Her father was a captain there in the regular British army. Before the war she used to spend her summer holidays with them in their bungalow in the hills. She'd come back with stories of tigers and tiger hunts, of her ayah who'd been her nurse for years and years, of mosquitoes and heat and flies, and all the romantic faraway things we could never imagine in dull, rainy Belfast. But since the war there'd been no traveling. Lizzie Mag was stuck here, even on holidays.

Miss Müller was in my doorway now. She looked around my room to check that I'd obeyed all the air-raid regulations. My gas mask hung on the knob of my iron bed. My heavy coat and shoes were on my chair, ready to take with me. My flashlight with its new, strong batteries was on my dresser.

"Is your emergency suitcase prepared also?" Miss Müller asked.

6

I nodded.

"How was your father when you saw him, Jessie?"

"Very well, thank you," I said stiffly.

"Sleep tight, dear."

My door closed. Miss Müller always asked about my father. I'd told everyone he had a mysterious illness because they knew how much I worried after holidays and when I got letters from home. Once I'd been crying after lights-out, softly, secretly, and Miss Müller came and sat on the floor by my bed and stroked my hair and whispered to me not to cry. That everything would be all right. She was wearing her black silk dressing gown and she'd smelled of apricots. I thought she must use apricot soap.

Her own father was dead, Miss Müller told me. Fathers were so precious and she missed hers so much. She told me she'd been born in Berlin, but her mother was Irish. After her father died, they thought they should come back here, for her mother had once been a boarder at Alveara herself, years and years ago. Miss Müller's voice went on, soft and comforting. I knew she was just talking to keep me company. Just staying there being my friend.

"I am so fortunate to work here," she'd whispered. "What would my mother and I have done otherwise? This way I am able to live here and pay the rent for her little apartment. Not too many schools would hire someone as a teacher who's half German—not with the war on."

I think it was because of that talk that I always stuck up for Miss Müller.

The overhead lights clicked off. "Good night, girls,"

Miss Müller called. Her footsteps went toward her room, not toward the outside corridor and teachers' lounge. She was going to bed already.

"Tomorrow night we do it," Ada said in a loud voice. "Tonight's not going to work."

"No talking please, girls," Miss Müller called.

The dorm was quiet. Usually we jabbered for hours after lights-out, always on the alert for the shouted word "Dicks" that echoed from dorm to dorm and was the signal that a teacher or a prefect was on her way down the corridor. We told ghost stories and played Truth or Dare with squirming worries about the boy boarders and kissing and other things we weren't too sure about, but loved to imagine. We talked about Pearl Carson, who had a reputation for being "fast," and speculated on what exactly she did. After lights-out was always the best part of the day.

But not this day, since Miss Müller was staying around. Already Ada would be under her covers with her flashlight, reading.

Soon Maureen would start snoring. Her snoring was like a steamroller on a gravel path.

I lay watching the small lighted square of ceiling above Miss Müller's room. Our partition walls didn't go all the way to the ceiling, and hers didn't either. I used to be able to see the night sky, too, through the row of small, high windows that ran along the dorm. I'd think of my parents at home under the same moon and stars. The sky covered us all and brought us together. But now the blackout curtains were pulled tightly across the windows. A tram rattled past, bumping up the Lisburn Road on its metal tracks. Its windows would be painted black, too, the people inside like travelers in a dark ship on a dark sea.

I thought about the weekend at home, and a horrible rush of homesickness choked my chest. Why did my father promise me and promise me that he'd change and then break his word? Saturday had been awful. Remembering it, I couldn't sleep.

The mouse that came every night scampered across my floor. It rustled in the paper that had been around the chocolate.

Miss Müller's light went off.

The clock on the quad struck midnight. Its friendly face used to shine through my window, but now the window and the clock face were both dark.

I needed to go to the bathroom. It was awful to go to the bathroom at night all by myself, past the silent rooms. I was always scared. What if I met the ghost of Marjorie, the girl who had jumped from the Alveara roof years and years ago? People said her ghost slept up in the room we called the coffin room, or whispered itself along the corridors. But once I began thinking that I needed to go, there was no way to ignore it.

I got out of bed, took my flashlight, and went through the dorm. The bottoms of my slippers stuck to the floor at each step. The maids used polish on the linoleum and never rubbed it off. Maureen's snoring stopped for a moment when I tapped on her cubie wall, then started again full volume.

We shared the big bathroom with the girls from Sleeping Beauty and Cinderella. It crouched in the middle of the three dorms with its row of stalls, its lines of washbasins, and the three claw-footed tubs filled with cold

9

water in case an incendiary bomb fell in the night. Mr. Bolton, our Latin teacher, was our auxiliary fire-service officer. Two of the boy boarders helped, and Mr. Bolton had a mobile stirrup pump that he could wheel around in case of a fire. But the pump was kept outside the Latin room, and that was a long way from the girls' dormitories.

"You mean someone's supposed to grab one of those burning bombs and toss it in the bathtub?" Maureen had asked, raising her Arcs de Triomphe. "You're joking."

"It probably wouldn't be a joke if it happened," I said.

A blue light burned above the bathroom washbasins every night. If you peered into one of the mirrors you could scare yourself to death. Ada said you looked as if you'd been dead for a month already and the body snatchers had just dug you up.

I didn't flush when I was finished, because the tanks roared like Niagara Falls. I was out of the stall, padding under the blue light, my flashlight not on, when I saw Miss Müller. She was coming my way. Her head was bent and I knew she hadn't seen me.

For some reason I stepped back. It was daft to step back, because she had to be coming into the bathroom and she'd see me, hiding like an idiot behind the door.

But maybe she wouldn't see me.

She was carrying her flashlight, but she didn't have it switched on either.

I waited, trying to think of a strong story in case she did notice me. "I thought you were Marjorie's ghost, Miss Müller," I'd say. But she didn't come into the bathroom after all.

I peered through the crack between the door and the

wall and saw her leave the dorm and go up the two steps to Long Parlor. She still didn't switch on her light, though ahead of her Long Parlor would be dark as pitch. Her black robe and her mass of long black hair blended perfectly with the shadows around her. Where was she going in the middle of the night?

As if to agree with me, the quad clock struck one A.M.

My head buzzed with thoughts of spies and Nazis and short-wave radios. Should I follow her? Should I? Should I do it for the war effort, just in case?

I slipped from behind the bathroom door and moved silently behind her.

2

I FOLLOWED MISS Müller through Long Parlor and along the corridor that passed the teachers' lounge and, farther on, the dining room. She was in the front hall of Alveara now, and I was hidden in the shadows behind her, listening to the faint creaks as she went up the main staircase. Where was she going? Blackness crowded in on me, hiding the gold-framed portraits of former headmistresses that lined the walls. Still I felt their cold eyes watching me.

"Who is this girl?" I imagined one of them asking. "What's she up to?"

"Please, ma'am," I heard myself replying, "I'm following Miss Müller. I'm trying to find out if she's really a Nazi spy."

At the top of the stairs was only Nursie's dispensary, her bedroom, and the sanitarium—the infirmary where we had to stay if we got mumps or measles or chicken pox. Nobody was sick right now, so both the san and the dispensary were locked at night. There was nothing else up there except the big stone archway with the narrow winding steps that led to the roof. This was the roof that Marjorie had jumped off long, long ago.

The steps wound past the coffin room that was locked to keep in Marjorie's ghost, we'd heard, as if a ghost can be kept anyplace it doesn't want to be kept. You could get expelled from Alveara if you as much as set foot on one of those steps. I expect they were afraid one of us would jump, too. And sometimes when we were mopey we threatened we would.

"It's me for the roof and the high jump," we'd say.

I peered through the darkness. There was no sound at all. Nothing.

Carefully, putting my weight more on the wide wooden banister than on the creaky stairs, I went up toward the second floor. The stairway carpet bristled under my feet. It was new carpeting, dark red, rough as horsehair.

"It makes the place look like a brothel," Ada had said.

"What's a brothel?" I'd asked.

"A house of ill repute."

"What's a house of ill repute?"

Ada didn't know for sure. None of us knew things like that for sure.

The landing above was dark as dark. The carpet changed there to cold linoleum. In Alveara if something couldn't be seen by visitors or parents, it was always done cheap. My teeth were rattling. Where was Miss Müller?

I felt along, past the dispensary and san doors, pressing myself against the bare whitewashed wall, hunching my shoulders, listening.

Was Miss Müller going to the roof? Why? She had that big flashlight with her. Dit-da-dit. Dit-da-dit. It would have a beam like a searchlight.

I went to the stone archway and looked up. The steps

13

to the roof wound round and round, narrow on the inside, widening toward the wall. Ahead of me was a shaded gleam. Its white shadow lightened the wall, disappearing as the steps curved, then appearing again farther up. Miss Müller's flashlight.

My feet were ice. Shivers ran up and down my legs. I couldn't go after her. No. I couldn't go up those steps without putting on my flashlight. I'd fall, or I'd die of fright there, especially passing the coffin room.

I couldn't.

Soundlessly I turned back the way I'd come, knowing where Miss Müller had gone, hurrying, filled with panic. Expecting hands to reach for me. Expecting Marjorie. Not knowing what I expected.

Dit-da-dit. A spy. The rhythm tapped itself inside my skull.

The light from my flashlight jumped in front of my slippers.

A cockroach scuttled into a crack in the corridor wall.

Quick, quick. Through Long Parlor. I bumped the Ping-Pong table and the balls rattled off, bounced on the floor.

Snow White dorm. I'd never heard anything as wonderful as Maureen's snores. She even muttered something in her sleep, and her mattress creaked as she turned over.

I was back. I was safe.

I opened Lizzie Mag's door.

She lay tidily in the bed, her sheet not even rumpled. Lizzie Mag is the tidiest girl in the whole world.

I touched her shoulder. "Lizard. Wake up. It's Jess," I added because my voice didn't sound like me.

14

She opened her eyes.

"Move over," I whispered, and wriggled in next to her.

With my mouth close to her ear I told her about following Miss Müller. "Right now she's probably up there on the roof signaling to German planes," I said.

"Oh, Jess. I can't believe it. Couldn't she have gone up for some other reason?"

"Marjorie went up there to jump," I said, and Lizzie Mag's hand tightened on mine.

"No," I whispered. "I was just joking. But something's not right."

My frozen feet had found Lizzie Mag's hot-water bottle at the bottom of her bed. It was still beautifully warm. We filled our bottles from the big boiling urn that was left for us in the kitchen at night, and they stayed hot till morning if we didn't kick them out of bed.

"Should you tell?" Lizzie Mag asked.

"You mean tell Old Rose?" My heart quaked at the thought. Old Rose Hazelton, our headmistress, was beyond-belief scary. "Do you think I should?" I was quaking all over. "If I do, maybe Old Rose will fire her," I said. "Even if there's a suspicion, Old Rose would probably fire her."

I thought about the night Miss Müller had come into my room. I thought about her voice and how gentle she'd been with me. "I am so fortunate to work here. What would my mother and I have done otherwise? . . . Not too many schools would hire someone as a teacher who's half German." No one would hire her if she were fired from Alveara. And what had she done, after all? Maybe she'd just gone up on the roof to get some air.

15

I nudged the hot-water bottle up and held it against my stomach.

"We could tell Maureen and Ada, and we could watch Miss Müller, the four of us," Lizzie Mag said. "We could take it in turns, staying awake at night."

"We could keep a record of where she goes and what she does," I said. I felt better. "That's a great idea, Lizzie Mag."

This way I'd be sharing what I knew, and it would be almost like a game—a spying game. If Miss Müller turned out to be innocent, there'd be no harm done. And if she wasn't . . . well, we'd face that if it happened.

3

Lizzie Mag dropped off to sleep and I crept back to my own cold bed. It was after two in the morning and I hadn't heard Miss Müller come back to her room. Some time later I fell asleep myself.

Morning bell wakened me. The sixth formers had to take turns staggering through the dorms every morning at half past six, swinging the bell on its long wooden handle. The noise was deafening. Immediately thoughts of Miss Müller crowded my mind. I remembered last night—the gleam of her flashlight moving up the stone steps toward the roof.

But why was the morning bell clanging like this? The bare-bulb dorm lights were on, and girls were screaming. And there was another sound, just as loud but different, a sound of wailing that came from outside.

Oh, no. That was the city air-raid siren, and I realized suddenly that the bell ringer was croaking at the top of her voice, "Air raid! Air raid!"

I fumbled out of bed. Next door Lizzie Mag was calling my name.

Doors banged and muddled voices called instructions.

17

We'd never had an air raid before. Practices, but never the real thing.

Someone was yelling orders from the front of the dorm. It was Miss Hardcastle, the gym teacher, whose room was in Cinderella.

"Put on your coats and shoes. Bring your cases, flashlights, gas masks. You know the drill. Come on now, girls, move quickly, don't panic."

The outside howling rose and fell like the cry of some sort of wounded beast. Every Friday at noon we heard this siren. We stuffed our ears and paid no attention. But we'd never heard it in the middle of the night before.

I had my coat on. I struggled into my shoes, found my case under the bed, pulled it out. Criminy. This case was filled with things that shouldn't be in it—movie magazines, my crystal-set radio, the photos of Ian McManus that Nancy Eden, a sixth former, had taken at a swimming meet. I was semi–in love with Ian McManus and I'd bought the pictures from Nancy for sixpence. To make room for all this I'd removed the emergency stuff from the suitcase, thinking I'd never need it. Now there was no use looking for clean underwear and socks and the things that were supposed to be in there. Maybe I could just . . .

There was a sudden whine like the whine of fireworks high in the sky. Then came an incredible bang that rattled the row of windows and made my brush and comb set jump from one side of the dresser to the other.

Everyone began screaming, "Bombs! Bombs!"

It was unbelievable. I had to be dreaming this. Were the Germans really bombing us?

A shrill, cutting *peep*, *peep* sliced through the uproar. Miss Hardcastle was blowing the gym whistle that she wore on a string around her neck. "Line up, now," she called. "File quietly along the corridor to the basement stairs. Stay by the left wall."

There was another loud boom. Somebody screamed.

I'd never heard a bomb fall, but there was no mistaking what this was. My stomach began to cramp and I doubled over. My stomach always cramps when I'm scared or nervous. I'd never been this scared.

Now I could hear gunfire. Sharp little faraway pops like someone cracking her knuckles. They must be midget guns.

Lizzie Mag burst into my room. "Hurry, Jess. Come on."

I snatched up my suitcase, grabbed Lizard's hand, and ran.

Ada and Maureen were already in line, along with some of the girls from the Cinderella and Sleeping Beauty dorms. They all had the same dazed, frantic look. Miss Hardcastle held up her hand and I saw that it was shaking, though her voice was calm. "Where's Daphne?" she asked.

Lizzie Mag stared at me. "Did Miss Müller not come back?" she whispered. "Oh, Jessie."

Maureen Campbell turned around and said, "Hitler probably warned her about this. She's probably safe in a shelter already."

"Sh!" Lizzie Mag said. "Hardcastle will hear." But Miss Hardcastle was too busy to be listening to us.

"Don't be so daft, Maureen," I muttered. But I was thinking muddled, scary thoughts. Miss Müller with her flashlight heading up to the roof. Planes over Belfast.

Lizzie Mag nudged me. "They couldn't pick her off

the roof, could they? They wouldn't be able to land and take off—"

EeeeeeeBANG! Another bomb.

We screamed, covering our heads with our arms. I didn't care about Miss Müller anymore. I didn't care about anything.

"Bengie!" Miss Hardcastle yelled. "Go back to Miss Müller's room. See if she's all right. I have to get these girls to the shelters. Hurry now."

Bengie was a prefect in Sleeping Beauty. Her real name was Sheila Bengers, but everyone called her Bengie. Every dorm except Snow White had a prefect as well as a mistress. Prefects were specially chosen sixth formers with responsibilities and some privileges, too. But Snow White was so small we didn't need a prefect, which made it nice.

Bengie looked now as if she might argue, but even with bombs falling, nobody argued with Miss Hardcastle.

"Move along, girls. March."

We cringed forward, waiting for the next bang that might be right here, right where we were walking, right on top of us. Lizzie Mag clung to my hand. "I want my ayah," she whispered. The clips had come out of her pin curls, and little loops of hair stuck up all over her head. She could have been four years old.

"It's okay, Lizard," I soothed, and soothing her made me feel better too.

We were halfway along the corridor when Bengie caught up with us. She ran to Miss Hardcastle.

"Miss Müller's not in her room," she said solemnly. I squeezed Lizzie Mag's hand.

"Should we say?" she whispered.

I shook my head. "Not now."

Miss Hardcastle was frowning. "Very well, Bengie. You go to the back of the line and bring up the rear."

I could tell Bengie didn't want to do that either. She wanted to run and be the first one to get into those shelters. I didn't blame her. But she did as Miss Hardcastle said.

Another stream of girls from the fifth-form dorm straggled ahead of us, and on the right-hand side was a column of little second formers, crying hard, calling for their mummies. Another bomb fell, but it was closer, louder. The whole of Alveara seemed to shake.

"It's all right, girls, just keep moving." Miss Hardcastle's voice was steady, but I knew the steadiness was fake. She was like the captain when the ship's going down, trying to be brave so everyone else would be brave too.

We were tripping over one another to get to those shelters. The locks on someone's case burst open and clothing fell out.

"Leave it, leave it," Miss Hardcastle shouted.

I could see the dining-room door and the basement steps that stretched down beside it. Coming in the other direction from the boys' wing were the boy boarders, their pajama legs wrinkled under their Burberry raincoats, their gas masks in cases just like ours. I'd never thought of them as like us in any way. It took my mind off my stomach. Boy boarders in the middle of the night? It was almost as incredible as an air raid.

The girls' lines and the boys' lines met at the basement steps, and there was Old Rose herself in her tatty fur coat, her hair rolled in metal curlers, shouting directions.

"Mr. Atkinson, hold your boys back," she called. Mr. Atkinson was headmaster of the boys' school. "Little girls first, down the stairs now. Nobody push. We are in no danger." Old Rose waved her arms like a traffic policeman.

"What does she mean, 'no danger'? Is the woman mad altogether?" Maureen hadn't penciled in her eyebrows and she looked like a fish. I felt like one.

Miss Gaynor was waiting at the bottom of the steps. "Each of you put your case on a bunk. Sit quietly beside it. Be orderly." Miss Gaynor was our domestic economy teacher. She was famous for making the worst scones. Bombs, we called them, as we tossed them into the wastebasket. We'd never joke about bombs again. Never.

Canvas bunks lined the basement walls. Lizzie Mag and I took two that were side by side. Everything smelled musty. The gray blankets folded on the bunks were damp—wet, even. It was dim as a cave with only two hanging yellow bulbs strung on two wires. Voices echoed.

"Are you okay, Lizard?" I asked softly.

She nodded. Strange how she'd wanted her ayah and not her mum. Once she'd whispered to me that she loved her ayah more than anybody in the world. "Except you, Jessie. And my mother and father, of course," she'd added.

Big bottles of water stood between the rows of bunks. Shovels and picks leaned in a corner. In case we have to dig out, I thought. And I imagined us, the concrete ceiling fallen on top of us. Tables and chairs, too, because wasn't the dining room right above our heads?

But there hadn't been a bomb for a while now, and it felt safe down here. It felt like a place the Germans

22

couldn't get to. There was a big white chest close to us with a Red Cross emblem on its side. That would be for the bandages and the iodine in case anyone got injured.

And there was Nursie. I hardly recognized her in her gray-checked dressing gown instead of her stiff, white uniform. Nursie fixed all our complaints with milk of magnesia for our insides, iodine for our outsides. She had a long horse face and a horse-whinny laugh. She was not laughing tonight.

Looking past Nursie, I saw that all the boarding mistresses were here now—but not Miss Müller.

"Maybe it's over," Lizzie Mag said. "I don't hear anything."

"Maybe. Or maybe you don't hear when you're down in the shelters."

I was thinking now about my mother and father. The Germans would never bomb our little town of Ballylo, would they? They probably didn't even know it was there, with just thirty houses and the church and school and the four pubs. It wasn't even on the map of County Derry, not unless you looked at a big, detailed one. Would my mum and dad know what was happening in Belfast tonight? They might even hear the bombs falling. If they did, they'd be scared out of their minds about me.

Greta Ludowski sat alone on the bunk next to us. She leaned against the wall, and I thought she was half smiling. Greta was Polish. She had been smuggled out by her parents when the Nazis invaded their country in 1939. Greta had been through so much, she probably thought this air raid was nothing. She probably thought we were a bunch of rabbits even to be scared.

"Jess." Lizzie Mag dug an elbow into my side and

23

wiggled to the edge of her bunk. "Here come the boys," she said.

I forgot about Greta Ludowski. We stared at the boys as they straggled along with the boarding masters. Mr. Stinky Larrimer, who taught chemistry and always walked with his nose twitching as if he smelled a bad smell; plump, dear Mr. Bolton with his round face and round glasses, always nice, especially polite to the girls. His Burberry was wet, his glasses misted with rain. I guessed he'd been out to the shed by the Latin room to get his stirrup pump in case of a fire. There was Mr. Guy, who taught English and was handsome as anything. When he read romantic poems by Robert Browning or Swinburne, we swooned away. We dreamed about Mr. Guy falling in love with one of us, deserting his wife and two children.

"It could happen. Jane Eyre was a lot younger than Mr. Rochester," Ada assured us.

"But it's not too likely."

"What a 'guy,' " we'd say, and dream on.

Mr. Guy looked pale and sick tonight, probably from worrying about his wife and children in Bangor, not too far from Belfast as the crow flies. Or the Germans.

Some of the boys grinned bravely at us as they passed. I could feel us all perk up. Usually we saw the boys only in class or at mealtimes, and if we were caught talking to them, well, it was big trouble. And here they were in the almost dark, close enough to touch. They were real now; the air raid wasn't.

"There's Ian," Lizzie Mag whispered.

I was watching for him. His name was the one I muttered in the dorm after lights-out when we played Truth or Dare. "Which boy do you like best, Jessie?"

"Ian McManus," I'd say, my face squished hot against my pillow. I definitely wouldn't have paid sixpence for anybody else's picture. Especially since we saved all our pocket money to buy war bonds.

I tried to smooth down my hair, something which is just never possible. There he was, not tall, dark, and handsome, the way the movie magazines describe movie stars—more like medium tall, blondish, but definitely handsome. Ian had gray eyes, a sharp little chin, and a beauty mark at the side of his mouth. Some people might call it a mole, but Lizzie Mag and I decided it was definitely a beauty mark.

"He looks glamorous even in the middle of an air raid," Lizzie Mag whispered.

I nodded. For a minute we forgot about bombs or being killed or injured.

I saw Ada's brother, Jack, tramping in carrying his case. He and Ada looked so alike, they could have been twins. But they weren't. Lizzie Mag once said a giant must have put a hand on each of their heads when they were born and pushed down. Even their legs were a little bendy, and their heads were perfect ovals, like rugby balls. They even had identical dimples in their chins. They waved to each other as Jack passed.

"Look," Lizzie Mag whispered. I looked and saw Miss Müller. She was wearing her black silky dressing gown, her black pajamas, and her black slippers with the little silver beads on them. Lizzie Mag and I were so close, we could hear Old Rose's voice, cold now and accusing.

"I understand you were not in your room when the air-raid siren sounded, Daphne."

Miss Müller faced Old Rose with her head up. "When the sirens started I remembered we had made no provision for the safety of Boots." Miss Müller paused, then added, "Boots, the caretaker who is deaf."

"I know very well who Boots is. Go on." Old Rose was making no effort to speak softly, and everyone was listening.

"I knew he would be unable to hear the sirens," Miss Müller said, "so I simply ran as quickly as I could to get him and bring him here." She pointed. "Poor old man. Indeed he had not heard. I had to shake him to get him awake."

Old Rose and Lizzie Mag and I and all the mistresses and just about everybody within hearing distance turned to look. Boots sat on the last bunk. He looked dazed. His gray hair stood on end and his hands dangled between his striped-pajamaed knees.

"That was very commendable, Daphne." Old Rose's voice was warmer, and she actually put a hand on Miss Müller's shoulder.

"Do you think Miss Müller really did go for him?" Lizzie Mag whispered to me.

I nodded. "Maybe. When she came down from the roof. But it still doesn't explain why she was up there in the first place."

Maureen had opened her case and was rooting through it.

"Do you know what time it is?" I asked her. She shook her head.

Ada, who wore her watch night and day, said, "It's twenty past four."

"In the morning?" Maureen asked.

"No," Ada said sarcastically. "In the afternoon."

"Oh." Maureen had found the mirror she'd been searching for and her soft 2B pencil. She drew in her arches and carefully rubbed a little Tangee lipstick over her mouth.

I thought back to before the air raid. I didn't know what time I'd drifted off to sleep, but Miss Müller had been gone for hours. It would have taken her only five minutes, maybe ten, to go to Boots's quarters.

I looked at her sitting there in her black dressing gown, blending into the shadows behind the hanging yellow bulbs. Up on the roof against the night sky, she would have been invisible, except for the light from her flashlight. Dit-da-dit. Dit-da-dit. And the sky itself dark with German planes.

"Don't you think it was a bit of a coincidence that Miss Müller was up on the roof on the very night we had our first air raid?" Lizzie Mag whispered.

"Yes," I said. "A bit of a coincidence."

4

A LOUD, ONE-NOTE wail, long and earsplitting, sounded from outside. The all-clear. We heard it on Fridays at five minutes past noon, so we recognized it right away.

"The all-clear," Old Rose called, in case we were too far gone to remember how it had sounded in the practices. She was standing on the bottom step, beaming down on us. "We shall have to give heartfelt thanks to the Almighty at morning prayers." Old Rose had been in amateur dramatics when she was a girl, and she never missed the chance to declaim.

We jumped off the bunks, cheering and clapping and hugging one another. "It's over. It's over."

Someone started singing, "We're gonna hang out the wash on the Siegfried Line." It was a Gracie Fields song that made fun of the Germans' first line of defense, which was supposed to be so strong nobody could get through it. And suddenly the boys came rushing up, singing and cheering too.

There was a new frosty note in Old Rose's voice. "Children, children. This is not the way to behave. Get into orderly lines, girls at the front, boys at the back."

Too late. We were squashed together in the shelter like

28

bananas in a bunch and we were mingling. Mingling in our pajamas. They were under our coats, of course, but still we were in our pajamas. It was the most astonishing part of the whole astonishing night.

Old Rose was standing on the big Red Cross box now, tottering a bit, holding on to Miss Gaynor's shoulder. Her face was flushed with fury. "Mr. Atkinson, control your boys."

And then, with a little hiss and a squeak, the basement lights went out.

There was a moment of silence and the noise doubled. The boys surged closer to us and we surged closer to them. There was more mingling than any of us had ever dreamed of.

In the dark it was hard to tell boy boarder from girl boarder, except by the feel of the coats. Ours were woolen, soft and prickly. Theirs were Burberrys, smooth, slick raincoats.

"Who's this?" I asked, my fingers slithering across the lapels of someone's Burberry.

"It's Curly Pritchard. Who's this?"

"Jessie Drumm."

"Hiya, Jessie." He grabbed me and tried to kiss me, but I turned my head so he got my ear. Curly Pritchard was in my geography class. He was a twerp and a sneak. Just my luck to get him.

"Where are you?" he growled. "What part of you was that?"

"I'm gone," I told him, stepping back on somebody's toes.

Teachers' flashlights clicked on and roamed across the mass of pushing, trampling boarders. None of us was daft

29

enough to put on *our* flashlights and spoil the first good, dark mingling we'd ever had. Even the little first and second formers were giggling and singing, "We're gonna hang out the wash on the Siegfried Line, Have you any dirty washing, Mother dear?"

Old Rose's voice shrieked through the noise, accompanied by the all-clear, which was still wailing outside. Either it was supposed to go on a long time, or it was stuck.

"I will not have this," Old Rose screamed. "This is a serious, life-changing experience."

It surely was. Us and the boys.

"Each one of you climb onto a bunk and stay there," Old Rose shouted.

From out of the dark a boy's voice called, "Lie down quietly. One boy and one girl to each bunk, please."

Old Rose sounded as if she was having a conniption fit. "Who said that? Mr. Atkinson, I demand to know which of your boys made that ugly suggestion. I want him severely punished."

"I'm sorry, Miss Rose. I have no way of ascertaining," Mr. Atkinson said.

"Boys." That was Mr. Bolton. "Please remember you are gentlemen."

And then Mr. Guy. "Come on, boys, relax. Let's behave."

His flashlight slid across a scene that looked like the Saturday-night dance at the Palladium without music.

I caught a glimpse of Ada next to me. "Isn't this great?" she said. "It's the first good thing Hitler's done in the whole war."

Another flashlight swung in our direction, and for a

miraculous second I saw Ian McManus right in front of me. I was looking into his eyes. He was looking into mine. I was closer to his beauty mark than I'd ever been before. My heart turned over and my stomach, too. If my stomach acted up on me now, I'd never forgive it.

And then Ian's face came forward, or mine did. Our gas mask cases that hung from our shoulders banged together with a metallic thump. Our noses bumped, but not enough to hurt, and Ian kissed me.

That kiss was right on target, but so fast and so light we could have been two butterflies meeting in midair. It was wonderful, but skimpy for a first kiss.

I didn't step away. Maybe there'd be a repeat that would be even more romantic. Ian might take my face in his hands and say, "I've been wanting to kiss you since the first time I saw you at the Pride of Erin dance when we were both in lower second."

He said nothing like that.

"Oh, cheese. Wouldn't you know it," he muttered, because right then the lights sparked and came on again.

Our eyes were still locked in love.

I smoothed my hair. I was so glad I didn't have cold cream on my face—or worse, the potter's-clay mask for pimples that Phyllis Hollister wore every night and offered to share. She'd wiped hers off on the way down here, but I noticed that some clay was still stuck under her chin and in her ears. I'd have died if Ian and I had been this close and I'd had potter's clay in my ears.

I smiled at him, but he looked embarrassed and stepped behind Curly Pritchard.

Old Rose was booming in her most Shakespearean voice, "Girls, are my eyes deceiving me? Is this conceivably possible?" She was back on the Red Cross box, and the hairs on her fur coat stood straight out like a mad dog's. "Never did I expect to see my girls—my Alveara girls— behaving in such a shocking manner."

Cowed, we stepped back and perched on the edges of bunks, while the boys, caught in the wrong place at the wrong time, looked nervous.

"First- and second-form teachers, Miss Hardcastle, Miss Gaynor, Miss Müller, the air raid is over. Bring my girls back to the dormitories." Old Rose paused. "Now."

We streamed awkwardly toward the stairs. Half of us had forgotten or lost our suitcases.

"Never mind, never mind," Old Rose called when Nancy Eden started back for her case. "The staff will gather up your belongings later."

Pearl Carson, for some reason, seemed to have also lost her coat.

Lizzie Mag and I had been separated. She was way up the line ahead of me, but I couldn't wait to give her my news. Maureen was in front of me. I tapped her shoulder. "I was kissed," I whispered. "Pass it on to Lizzie Mag."

Maureen gave me an over-the-shoulder arched- eyebrow look. "That's no news," she said. "Lots of us were kissed."

I felt like telling her my kiss was from Ian McManus and the other kisses were ordinary. But I didn't. And then I couldn't stand not to tell and I said, "Ian McManus kissed me."

"You're joking," Maureen said. "Lucky."

Miss Müller stood at the bottom of the steps with Nursie. I didn't want to look at her. Inside my head I asked, Where were you? Where were you really?

32

I had one foot on the bottom stair when Nursie caught my arm. "Jessie Drumm, are you all right?" She felt my forehead and frowned.

Miss Müller smiled at me and said, "It was a frightening experience, Nursie. None of us is all right."

I gave her my coldest glance. Don't even talk to me, I thought. Don't be my friend.

Nursie was peering closely into my face. "You're very flushed, Jessie. I want to see you in dispensary in the morning. Is your stomach bothering you?"

Thank heaven the boys were out of hearing. Imagine her mentioning one of my body parts like that. Of course I'd been to the dispensary and had had more than my share of milk of magnesia. So Nursie knew all about my weak intestines, as she called them. She patted my shoulder. "Morning dispensary," she said again.

"Yes, Nursie."

I was looking down at Miss Müller's black beaded slippers and then at old Boots, who had shuffled off to the side. I could see his heavy brown shoes clearly. They were thick with wet mud, and the bottoms of his pajamas, too. I remembered that right in front of the steps next to his caretaker quarters there was a dip where muddy water collected after it rained. It rained just about every day, so that mud puddle was always there.

If Miss Müller had gone to Boots's quarters as she'd said, gone in, shaken him awake . . . I looked again at her black slippers. They were dry and there wasn't a bit of mud on them. Even that part of what she'd said wasn't true. She hadn't gone near Boots's quarters. She had been up on the roof all the time, and of course old Boots wouldn't contradict her. He wouldn't even have heard what she'd said.

"I'll check on you girls later, back in the dorm," Miss Müller said.

I didn't answer.

We tripped up the stairs and along the corridor, everyone talking a mile a minute. Nobody seemed to notice that Lizzie Mag and I weren't joining in.

"Can't you be quiet, you monsters?" Miss Hardcastle asked, but not as forcefully as she usually does. "You all did well tonight. I'm proud of you."

"It was fun," Maureen said.

"It wasn't fun for everyone," Miss Hardcastle said. "Those bombs did damage somewhere in Belfast. I expect people were killed."

That made us settle down.

"Do you think they came over Belfast by mistake?" Maureen asked. "Like they were heading someplace else and got lost?"

"I doubt that very much," Miss Hardcastle said.

When we got back to the dorm, we gathered in Lizzie Mag's room. For a little while we talked in hushed voices.

"I suppose some people *were* killed," Lizzie Mag said. "How awful."

Maureen, who was checking her lipstick in the mirror, said: "Somebody grabbed me and kissed me and put his hand here." Her fingers fluttered between her chest and her dangling gas mask.

"It's nice that you're so worried about people getting killed, Maureen," I said.

34

She gave me a surprised Arcs de Triomphe look. "What's the point in thinking about such awful things when there are such good things to think about?" she said.

"Maybe the person who grabbed you had a cold and he was looking for one of the handkerchiefs in your bra," Ada suggested. "Maybe he needed to blow his nose."

"Jealous, jealous," Maureen said. "And Jessie was lucky too. Ian McManus kissed her, remember?"

I could feel my face getting hot.

"Was it great?" Ada asked.

It was half a relief and half a disappointment when Miss Müller called from the front of the dorm, "Is everyone in bed?"

"Almost, Miss Müller."

We scampered.

"It's about five in the morning," she said. "The planes have all gone."

"The German planes?" Ada asked, as if Miss Müller had thought it had been English planes bombing us. For once Ada's sarcasm didn't irritate me. Miss Müller had it coming.

"Try to get some sleep," Miss Müller said. "They won't be back tonight."

"She should know," Maureen's whisper was loud enough for us to hear. For Miss Müller to hear, too.

"Good night," Miss Müller said firmly.

I heard the little sliding sound her slippers made on the linoleum floor as she went to her room.

"Miss Müller," I called out. "Did you take Boots back to his quarters? You went and got him when the air raid started, didn't you? Didn't you?" I asked, repeating it in the same kind of sarcastic voice Ada had used.

There were a few seconds of silence; then Miss Müller said, more sharply than she had ever spoken to me before: "He went back by himself, Jessie. Old Boots is deaf, not blind."

"Yes, thank you. I know that," I said. My heart was thumping. I lay in the darkness that was total except for the ceiling glow from Miss Müller's lamp. I'd had my first air raid tonight, and my first kiss. I remembered Ian's lips, so soft and dry. They'd made me tingle. I was tingling now.

Tonight I'd had my first real suspicions about Miss Müller, too. I shuddered a bit and turned over in bed.

5

THEY LET US sleep an hour later than usual the morning after the air raid. I heard first bell, saw my emergency case where I'd dropped it in the middle of the floor when we came back last night, and remembered everything. I lay thinking about my mother and father. Were they all right? Oh, please, they had to be all right.

"Are you awake, Jess?" Lizzie Mag called.

"Sort of," I said.

"Did all those things really happen?" she asked, and her head bobbed up over the top of the partition that divided our cubies. We could do that if we stood on our dressers.

"I think so," I said.

She and I walked to the bathroom together carrying our soap dishes and towels and our still-warm hot-water bottles.

"When are you going to tell Maureen and Ada about Miss Müller?" Lizzie Mag whispered.

"After school, I guess. There'll be no time before, not to give them the details. We could still start the spy watch tonight."

Some of the girls from the other dorms were in the bathroom already, all buzzing about the air raid.

A list of names and dates was pinned to the bathroom wall. Three of us were supposed to break the skimming of ice and bathe in one of the cold tubs every morning, so as not to waste water. My name was on for this morning, but I checked to make sure no one was looking, then crossed it off and pulled the plug.

Bengie stood at one of the washbasins. Usually we tried to avoid prefects. They tended to be bossy, and they were supposed to make us stick by the rules. But when we saw Bengie today, we crowded around her. The prefects had a radio in their sitting room and could get the BBC news.

"Did you hear anything about the air raid, Bengie?" The big cave of the bathroom made our voices hollow, as if we were talking through a pipe. The damp air smelled of disinfectant, Monkey Brand soap, and the hot-bicycle-tire smell of water that's been rumbling around in a dozen hot-water bottles all night.

"Thirteen people got killed," Bengie said.

We gasped. Thirteen people. How awful to think we'd been enjoying ourselves when people were dying.

"The Germans dropped six bombs," Bengie went on. "Most of the damage was done on the Shore Road."

"Do they think someone in Belfast guided the planes?" Lizzie Mag asked.

Bengie snorted. "If somebody did, he did a bad job. The bombs were probably meant for the shipyards, and they missed by a mile."

Lizzie Mag's eyes met mine in the mirror. The blue

38

lights were off for daytime, so we looked normal—not great but normal.

"Was there bombing anyplace else?" I asked. "In Derry?"

Ada interrupted me. "In Dungannon?" That's where her parents lived.

"No place else," Bengie said. "Only Belfast."

We all smiled.

"Whew!" Ada crossed herself, which was an awful thing to do since none of us was Catholic, but it did help to relieve the pressure.

"Did we manage to shoot down any of their planes?" I asked Bengie.

Bengie put her soap dish on the shelf above the line of basins. In the mirror we watched our own cluster of faces. Watched Bengie take off her dressing gown and roll up her pajama sleeves.

"Naah. We didn't get even one. The English took all the Irish anti-aircraft guns a while back. They didn't think we were important enough to ever be bombed."

"But we heard gunfire," Lizzie Mag said.

"Those were just ground guns. They couldn't shoot high enough to hit a sea gull."

"The nerve of those English," I said. "We could have shot down all the German planes last night if they'd left us our own property. The English are always taking our stuff."

"Well, at least we got to see the boys." Phyllis Hollister peered closely at herself in the mirror and peeled away a smudge of potter's clay that had lodged under her chin.

"I swear, Phyllis Hollister!" Bengie looked disgusted

that we would even be interested in seeing the boys, although I knew for a fact that she'd gone more than once behind the kindergarten huts with Gordon Craig, who was a boy prefect and who always played leading man in the school shows. We'd been told that only one thing went on there behind those kindergarten huts. Nobody told us exactly what that one thing was, but we knew it was strictly forbidden, even for prefects. Still, it was pretty disgusting for Phyllis to be talking about boys when all those people had been killed. Not thinking about boys would be impossible. Talking about them now just didn't seem right.

Bengie dried her face and arms and said casually, "Morning assembly will be very interesting today. There's going to be a sensation."

"A sensation? What, Bengie? What kind of sensation? You mean because of the air raid?" All of us spoke at once.

"Partly. You could say that."

I could feel my stomach tightening. Was the sensation about me? Was it because someone had seen me kissing Ian McManus? But lots of others had kissed too.

"You'll find out. Just don't miss assembly, that's all." Bengie wiggled her fingers over her shoulder at us as she departed.

"She's so mean not to tell us," Lizzie Mag said.

Ada nodded. " 'A little knowledge is a dangerous thing.' You know who said that?" she asked Maureen.

Maureen looked puzzled. "Was it one of our teachers?"

By then girls were drifting into the bathroom from the

other dorms, and all of them were talking about last night.

"Maybe the sensation's about Miss Müller," Lizzie Mag whispered. "Maybe she's been found out."

I emptied my hot-water bottle into one of the basins. The water made a small, lukewarm puddle that barely covered the stopper. If I added more water from the faucet, it would be freezing cold. "Maybe somebody else saw her," I whispered. "Oh, cheese, Lizard. I've been hoping and hoping she's innocent."

Mean Jean Ross, who wore a big silver crucifix around her neck, said, "It sounds as if somebody's head is going to be on the block this morning at assembly." When she said that, she smiled her Mean Jean smile. She loved it when someone got in trouble. Her father was a Methodist minister, but none of the holiness had rubbed off on her.

"We're hoping the head on the block will be yours," Ada told her, chopping down with one hand and running her finger across her throat.

"Really," Mean Jean said.

Second bell was trilling in the distance and we had to hurry. Lizzie Mag and I skipped washing and headed back to our cubies.

I got dressed quickly, fastening my narrow garter belt, pulling up my black stockings and navy-blue knickers. I hadn't opened this week's laundry parcel, so I ripped it apart now, shook the folds from my white blouse, and got my gym tunic from under the mattress, where I put it each night to keep the pleats in.

Getting dressed for the execution, I thought, and then suddenly I remembered. I had to go to Nursie's dispensary this morning after breakfast. I didn't dare skip it. It

41

was as much as your life was worth to ignore an order from Nursie. I'd hurry and hope I was first in line. Then I'd take whatever Nursie gave me and gulp it down fast.

Lizzie Mag was at my door.

"Coming," I said as I finished knotting my tie.

"I was thinking, if Miss Müller has been caught, we don't have to plan on watching her. Most likely she won't be around to watch." Lizzie Mag gave me a frightened glance.

I nodded.

We hooked arms and joined the others tramping up the corridor to the dining room just the way we did every morning. But this wasn't like every other morning.

Now we could see the boys coming toward us from their wing. A bunch of teachers in their floating black university gowns stood as usual at the dining-room doors. You would think nothing out of the ordinary had happened. No air raid, no bombs, no possible spies at Alveara, no kissing in the shelter.

"Boys to the left, girls to the right. Boys to the left, girls to the right," the teachers chanted as usual. And as usual they kept a close watch for love notes being passed. Outside the dining room was a favorite note-passing place.

Today I didn't see a single letter being confiscated. Actually, nobody had had time to write one, as we'd all had other things on our minds. We went to our places at the tables and stood behind our chairs with our hands folded and our eyes closed.

Mr. Atkinson said grace, and our voices joined in. "Sanctus, sanctus, sanctus Dominus Deus," we chanted.

I glanced through my half-closed eyes at Miss Müller

42

standing in her place at the head table with the other women teachers. Old Rose never appeared at breakfast. She said she meditated at the start of each day, but we knew for a fact she was just taking an extra hour in bed, probably snoring her brains out like Maureen.

Miss Müller looked pale and tired. Her dark-red lipstick matched the dark-red suit she wore under her black gown. Her eyes were closed. She must have known how we felt about the Germans this morning. And that almost everybody here detested her. Did she know about the sensation that was coming? She must. I glanced at her again. The muscles in the sides of her neck were tight. Maybe her teeth were clenched.

After grace and before we sat down, Mr. Atkinson gave a small P.S. of thanks that we had sustained no injuries last night, and prayed for those who had.

"Amen," we chanted.

Our chairs scraped across the floor as we pulled them out. We had place lists that changed every month, so we had to sit where we were told to. Ada said we'd have lists for our funerals when the time came. This month my back was to the boys and I had to depend on Lizzie Mag for commentary on Ian. Today we didn't even mention him, though. There were too many other things going on, which was sad, because a girl's first kiss should never be overshadowed by anything.

The maids came up from the kitchen carrying the trays filled with the thick slices of bread and margarine, the big white jugs of milk, and the boiled eggs in their shells.

I poured milk for all those around me, the way I always did. I loved milk when I was at home, but I didn't like it here. It smelled of the dishcloths they used in the

43

kitchen when they washed the jugs. Ada said the best thing to do was not to breathe when you drank.

There was a sudden sharp little scream from farther up the table.

"It's Carol Murchison," Ada said, craning her neck. "What's wrong with her?"

Carol was a prefect in Goldilocks. We all leaned forward and watched as she shoved back her chair and stood, her hands pressed to the sides of her face, her eyes staring down at the table.

"Heaven save us. Maybe there's a German under there," Nancy Eden screamed. "Maybe one bailed out and came down on his parachute!"

Girls were scraping out their chairs and lifting the tablecloth, trying to see beneath it. Others peered through the mullioned windows, where rain beat at the glass, making it impossible to see anything.

"Maybe we're being invaded," Nancy Eden shrieked.

Pat Crow, who sat next to Carol, yelled, "It's not the Germans. It's not an invasion. There's a dead chicken in Carol's egg." Pat held her nose and pointed.

Mr. Atkinson tapped his spoon against his cup and called, "Settle down, girls. What *is* the matter?"

Carol gulped. "There's a dead chicken in my egg, sir."

"Impossible. Bring it up here."

Carol ran her hands down the sides of her gym tunic and stepped back. "I can't, sir. I can't touch it, honestly."

The eggcup got shoved along the table and half a dozen girls managed to look in it before Miss Hardcastle came stomping over and picked it up.

"It's got a beak and everything," one of the girls said, gagging behind her napkin.

The boys guffawed and poked each other and made clucking sounds. Boys can be horrible sometimes. They think they're so superior.

"Such a commotion over nothing," Miss Hardcastle said severely. Then she looked into the egg herself, gasped, and turned a strange color. She held the eggcup at arm's length, went to the top of the kitchen stairs, and called, "Bridget? Mary?"

One of the new little maids came and took the eggcup away.

"Carol, would you like them to bring you another egg?" Miss Hardcastle asked.

"No, thank you, Miss Hardcastle. Not for the rest of my life," Carol said.

None of us wanted our eggs but Miss Gaynor said we must think of the starving children in Europe and not waste good food. Several of us told her we would have been happy to send the starving children of Europe every egg in Ireland.

Nobody wanted to eat anything more, and we were glad when at last Mr. Atkinson stood to dismiss us. Usually he said, "Deo gratias, hosanna in excelsis." Today he added, "And don't let the Jerries get you down." We liked to call them Jerries instead of Germans. It made them sound less scary.

We all shouted, "They'll never get us down," and stamped our feet in approval.

The teachers left first, all of them except the two on inside dining-room duty. I watched Miss Müller. She walked with her head down and she was almost at the door when the hissing began. I don't know who started it, or even where it came from. One moment we were

45

cheering because the Jerries would never get us down, and then the cheering had changed to this ugly, hateful sound. It filled the dining room like steam coming out of a kettle. Miss Müller stopped, lifted her head, then bowed it again and walked faster.

Mr. Bolton moved beside her. He took her arm and bent over her. His round face was kind and concerned. The short bulk of his body seemed to be shielding her from our attacks. Teachers always stuck together no matter what.

Mr. Atkinson turned to face us. "Stop this abominable noise at once," he said. His glare was so fierce that the hissing began to die away.

The kettle being taken off the stove, I thought numbly.

Mean Jean Ross's finger traced the shape of the silver cross under her blouse. She wasn't allowed to have it outside when she was wearing her gym tunic. She said she should be allowed, because it was God's symbol, but Old Rose said it was jewelry and no jewelry was permitted when we were in uniform.

"It's going to get worse for the Fräulein before it gets better," Mean Jean said with satisfaction.

I had a feeling Mean Jean was right.

6

WE DRIFTED ALONG the corridor away from the dining room.

"Let her pass *that* along to Hitler," Ada said, and went "sssssss" between her little squared-off teeth.

"Too bad it wasn't Miss Müller that got the egg," Maureen said. "That would have been true justice. A rotten egg for—"

I interrupted. "I have to go to dispensary and I'm rushing so I'll be there first. Save me a seat at the assembly, Lizzie Mag."

"Hurry," she called after me. "You don't want to miss anything."

"I'll go like the wind."

I ran up the stairs, remembering last night: the red brothel carpet, the painted portrait eyes watching me. Nightmare time! But when I turned to look, the eyes were still watching me. The past headmistresses were extra guards in our boarder prison, keeping an eye on our every move. I ran the last few steps to the dispensary.

Cheese! Even though I was out of breath from running, two other, younger girls had made it before me. They were leaning against the wall, talking about the air raid.

47

Opposite them the san door lay open. When there were no patients, Nursie unlocked the door every morning in case of emergency, though there'd never been one yet as far as I knew. To my right was the arched stone opening and the steps that led to the roof. Not so scary now in daylight, but scary enough.

"I was awful frightened by those bombs," the little girl ahead of me was saying to the other one. I remembered her name was Hillary something. Walker, I thought.

"Me, too," the girl in front of her said. She was wearing the badge on her tunic that showed she was on the under-ten hockey team. I thought her name was Flash. "A lot of the fifth and sixth formers seemed to be having fun," Flash said, and I knew her big-eyed innocent look was just a put-on. She meant I, for one, had been having fun. The two of them giggled and put their hands over their mouths. They wanted me to know they knew.

"Wasn't it awful the way everybody hissed Miss Müller this morning?" Flash asked me.

"She deserved it," little Hillary said quickly. "She's a Nazi. Her daddy was in the Nazi army."

"You don't know that," I said.

"I do too." Hillary stopped cat-scratching her back against the wall and stood straight. "Somebody told me. Somebody who knows. Dear Daphne even has a picture of her daddy that she keeps hidden in her room. He's wearing his uniform with a swastika on it and everything."

"Who's going to know about the photograph if it's hidden?" I asked.

48

The two looked at me as if ready to pounce. Little snigs.

"Flash, come in now," Nursie called from inside the dispensary.

"Uh-oh. Here goes nothing." Flash made a face.

I stood leaning against the wall with Hillary.

"Flash has a really bad blister on her heel," Hillary told me. "Nursie'll probably stick it with a needle and put on peroxide."

I nodded.

Hillary took a few steps away from me and pretended to study a crack in the wall.

"Who told you about that picture, Hillary?" I asked.

"Nobody." She didn't turn, and I saw how stiff her back was.

"Oh, come on, Hillary. You started this, and you said it in front of Flash. It isn't any big secret. You might as well tell me."

Hillary gave me a long-suffering look. "I'll be in trouble if Sarah finds out I told."

"Sarah?" I asked.

"Sarah Neely. The wee maid that cleans out our dorms?"

I nodded.

Hillary went on. "You know when I go home to Monaghan on the train for the holidays?"

I nodded again to encourage her, though I didn't know anything about Hillary.

"Well, Sarah's mum works for my mum in Monaghan, you know? And my mum always tells me to stay in the carriage with Sarah, because sometimes there are bad men that get in with you and say things, and show you things. I asked Mummy what things, but she wouldn't tell me." Hillary gave me a hopeful look, but I just shrugged.

"Which maid is Sarah?" I asked, bringing Hillary back to the present.

"She's the one that has all the pimples on her face. They're all over her shoulders, too. She let me see them on the train one time. Well, Sarah saw the photo herself. It's on Miss Müller's dressing table but hidden behind another one. The maids found it. Sarah says the maids find everything. She says you wouldn't believe the things the maids find in the boys' rooms under their mattresses. She says the maids have great giggles over them."

They probably knew about the picture of Ian McManus in my emergency case, I thought. And oh. My heart chilled. What about my diary? The one I wrote in about Daddy. The one I cried over.

Hillary was going on. "The maids all hate us, except Sarah likes me. They think we're spoiled brats. Imagine! I'd rather be a maid here than a boarder any day."

I nodded. There was a muffled squeak from the dispensary, and then Nursie's no-nonsense voice. We couldn't hear the words, but Hillary said, "Nursie's telling her to be a brave soldier. That's what she always says."

I stood thinking about Miss Müller and the Nazi photograph. Was it true? Maybe the maids had lied, just to create a sensation. Miss Müller hadn't told me her father had been in the Nazi army. But she wouldn't tell any of us that. And after all, I didn't tell everything about my father either.

I hunched my shoulders and looked at the archway, half expecting to see Marjorie's ghost there. I always half expected to see Marjorie's ghost, but I never had. Not yet. If I went up on the roof, would there be any clue to what Miss Müller had been doing last night—just before the Nazi planes came and bombed Belfast? Should I look?

"Hold my place," I told Hillary, and went slowly across to the archway.

"It's out of bounds up there," she called out to me, as if I didn't know.

I peered up the spiral staircase. Damp, dark, curving into the darkness.

Behind me Hillary pressed herself against the wall and gasped with excitement.

I went up. My shoes thumped on the stone steps that curved round and round. My heart thumped, too, as I moved past the coffin room. Usually, when I had to come up here on a dare, I edged as far from the coffin-room door as I could. I forced my toes to cling to the narrow steps, reached out to tap my fingers against the paneled wood, and croaked, "Marjorie, are you there?" We always had to do that on a dare.

This morning, though, I forced myself to grab the door handle and turn it. The hasp was chained and padlocked as usual. The long, thin, shield-shaped window beside the door let little light through its dirty leaded glass. Gray morning light filtered down from above. I went round and round, up and up, till I came to the opening and stepped out onto the roof.

Rain misted around me and puddles pocked the concrete roof. Above me the sky was dark and thick. I moved forward. Red-brick battlements, like rows of gappy teeth, protected the roof's edges. They were knee high where they joined, waist level at their tops. A person could hide behind one of these if he—or she—wanted to.

I looked around, searching for something. I wasn't sure what. All I saw were the wet Union Jack hanging up on the flagpole and the red buckets that the Air Raid Precaution people had filled with sand. Other buckets overflowed with water in case of fire. I stared over the battlements in the direction of downtown Belfast. A signal from this roof could have been seen anywhere in the city. When it wasn't misty or rainy you could see City Hall from here and the top of Robinson Cleavers, our biggest department store, and the Albert clock and the Cavehill. Sometimes you could even see the blue sheen of the water in the Belfast Lough.

I leaned forward. Weren't the clouds heavier where the Lough should be? A flame shot up. It took a minute for me to realize I was looking at the Shore Road, where last night bombs had fallen, where homes were destroyed and people killed.

I was cold, so cold. Rain soaked my blouse, sticking the long, white sleeves to my arms. I made myself look toward the Shore Road and thought, The Nazis did that. Maybe in some way Miss Müller had helped them. My stomach was cramping again, and I backed away from the roof's edge.

Carefully, I went back down the curved stone steps. A damp breeze seemed to follow me, to lift my hair. For a second I thought I smelled apricots, but it was probably my imagination. Up here near the coffin room you could imagine anything.

Hillary was still waiting at the dispensary. "I'm still

here," she said unnecessarily. "What can Nursie be doing to poor Flash?"

Hillary bobbed her head toward the stairs and rolled her eyes. Above the collar of her white blouse her neck was filthy. I could see the water mark where she'd washed the front of her face and for a couple of weeks forgotten there was a neck underneath. Poor little thing. There'd be no chance Nursie wouldn't notice it.

"Do you have a hanky?" I asked. She fished one out of her tunic pocket.

"Here, spit," I told her, and I tried to at least blur the line of dirt to blend with the rest.

"Thanks." She put the hanky back in her pocket. "Did you go past the coffin room?" she asked.

"It's not that bad," I said. "Sometimes I have to go up there for a dare." She would think that's why I'd gone today. I shivered, and she shivered along with me.

"I'd never," she said. "You're brave. I'd have a worm down my back first." A worm down your back was the penalty for not following through on a dare.

"You didn't see Marjorie, did you?" she whispered.

"No, thank goodness." I clenched my hands to stop my shivering.

"Nadine Porter saw her." Hillary's voice was so low I could hardly hear her.

"You mean she saw the ghost?"

Little Hillary nodded. "Nadine had the whooping cough. She was in the san, and in the middle of the night she started whooping awful bad."

I nodded. I'd had whooping cough myself.

"So she got out of bed and pressed the bell for Nursie. You know the bell by the door?"

53

I knew. It was under the light switch and it rang in Nursie's bedroom in case you needed her in the night. But you'd better really need her, or heaven help you.

"Well, Nadine rang and the door was open, the san door. 'Cause you know how Nursie likes it open when somebody's sick?"

"Yes, yes, go on."

"And Nadine said it's awful having to be in there with the door open, because Marjorie might come down, and there'd you be, sick and weak, and not able to scream, or even to run."

"Please, Hillary, will you just tell me?"

At that moment Flash appeared, one shoe off, limping.

"What did she do to you?" Hillary asked.

"You're to go in," Flash said.

"Did it hurt an awful lot? What she did to you?" Hillary whispered.

"It hurt like anything," Flash said, "and I had to keep my foot in disinfectant for ten minutes and then she put this big piece of wadding on it."

I grabbed Hillary's arm. "What do you mean Nadine Porter saw Marjorie's ghost?"

"She saw her going up the steps." Hillary was struggling to get her arm free. "Going back to the coffin room. I have to go. Nursie will be mad if I keep her waiting."

I held fast. "How did Nadine know it was the ghost she saw?"

"She was all in black and she was floating. Nadine told Nursie and Nursie said she was just having a bad dream. And gave her chamomile tea."

I felt the hairs on my neck prickle. Marjorie was everybody's bad dream.

54

Hillary had pulled her arm free.

"When was this?" I caught the girdle of her tunic and held fast. The girdle was like a sash, only thinner and longer.

"Let go," Hillary bleated.

Flash joined in. "You'd better let her go or I'm going to get Nursie."

"When was this?" I repeated.

"St. Patrick's Day. The cup final was on and Nadine didn't get to go. It was that night."

I let the girdle loose, and Hillary gave me an offended look and fixed her tunic pleats. "Honestly, you're really horrible, Jessie. Even if you did spit wash my neck."

"Hurry up in there," I said. "I want to get to assembly."

But I was thinking. St. Patrick's Day was two months ago. Something had happened that night. I tried to think back and then I remembered. There'd been a fire, a big one, down on the docks. Explosions, too. It had all been in the paper. Saboteurs—Fifth Column, they'd said. Munitions were stored there and somebody had pinpointed where they were. A spy.

A ghost had gone up the stairs that night. Nadine had seen her. It could have been the ghost of Marjorie—a shadow floating. I closed my eyes tight and heard my heartbeats strumming in my ears. A black dressing gown, black slippers, the black staircase. It could have been Marjorie. Or it could have been someone else. I hated to think so, but I knew it could have.

7

"SIGN IN, JESSIE," Nursie told me as soon as I opened the door. "How are the intestines this morning?"

"Very well, thank you, Nursie." I wrote my name in her big book. "I don't think I need—"

"Put the date, too, Jessie," she said over her shoulder as she went to her glass case and shook three milk of magnesia pills into her hand. Sometimes she gave us the liquid stuff in the blue bottle. It was like thick cream and was guaranteed to put you off our smelly milk for a week at least. Today she gave me the pills, which she said tasted like peppermint. She was joking.

I munched them with my front teeth, trying not to spread the chalk flavor. "Now, Jess, I don't want you to get yourself worked up worrying about another air raid," Nursie said. "The Germans have a lot more on their minds right now than bothering with us. There's terrible fighting in France, you know. The Jerries and our boys are having it out. Last night was just to let us know they haven't forgotten we're here."

"My cousin Bryan's in France," I told her. "It's awful scary to think he's in such a dangerous place."

Nursie gave me a look. "How do you know he's in

France? That's classified information. Loose talk costs lives."

"I know. Bryan would never talk loose. He sent us an air letter. It was all cut up by the censors. But we can tell by the BBC news that that's where all the fighting is."

Nursie turned back to lock the glass cupboard, and I pulled my stockings up tighter, which is something I did every time I got the chance. The most embarrassing thing was to have a space between the top of your stocking and the elastic of your knickers. Girls pointed and shouted, "Gaps! Gaps!" And you couldn't start fiddling around to fix them in the middle of the quad or someplace like that.

"Is there another girl waiting outside?" Nursie asked.

"No. I'm the last."

She patted my shoulder. "Don't you worry about your cousin, now. The British have ships waiting in case our boys have to get out in a hurry."

I ran my tongue over my chalky teeth and nodded. I tried not to worry, but to tell the truth I thought what Bryan was doing was exciting. I never thought of anything happening to him.

"Get yourself a glass of water before you go, Jess," Nursie said. She touched my sleeve. "Is your blouse wet?"

"Just a wee bit."

"Why on earth were you outside? Get down to your room this instant and change it, Jessie Drumm. You'll catch your death of cold."

"But Nursie . . ."

"Rush along, Jessie. Rush now."

I rushed, muttering to myself. Honestly, this morning of all mornings. I bounded down the stairs, not like a lady the way we're supposed to. Usually I wouldn't have minded being late for assembly, but today was different.

The dorm was empty. I unbuttoned my sleeves as I ran, unknotted my tie. As soon as I got into my room I pulled off my tunic, threw my wet blouse into my bottom dresser drawer, and found a clean one in my laundry pack. The dorm was strange without noise, without voices, without the sound of somebody playing the piano in the common room or the click click of Ping-Pong balls on the table in Long Parlor. Creepy, in a way.

We were never allowed back in our rooms between breakfast and assembly. "The maids must be free to do their jobs without interruption from you girls," Old Rose said.

I didn't think I'd ever been in the dorm alone before.

We're not like those maids, I thought, making a face at myself in the mirror. They were free. My diary. I got down on my knees and felt for it under my dresser. There was no private place in the dorm. Boarders weren't supposed to have secrets, that's why.

My fingers touched the small leather book and pulled it out. Hard to tell if anyone else had done this, even checked on me every day because I wrote every day. How awful. I opened the diary, flipped through the pages. Ian McManus's code letters jumped out at me: I'M, written like that. Those smart, horrible maids had probably decoded it by now. "I'M walked behind Ada and me to French class. He's had his hair cut short and he looks adorable." How embarrassing. Why had I written such a dopey thing?

I didn't have a code name for Daddy. There he was on almost every page, my thoughts about him, my rage. Last weekend I'd written in my diary, sitting here on my bed the night I got back to Alveara. "Went to Swatragh with Daddy. We were supposed to be going to see the Curragh bands. He left me in the car while he went into the pub to meet Jamie Ruck. I waited and waited. I read two stories from the new *Girls' Crystal*, my favorite magazine. Good thing I brought it. He didn't come back for more than an hour. 'Sorry, darlin',' he said. 'Jamie and I had important business to conduct.'

"He always gets so highfalutin when he's like that. I started to cry because I was so mad at him and nothing I say to him does any good. It's hopeless. 'What's the matter, darlin'? Sure there's no need to cry.'

" 'We've missed the bands,' I said, though I didn't care that much about hearing them. I was crying over him. But he's right. Crying is hopeless, too. Sometimes I don't love Daddy at all. I hate him."

I closed the diary and ran my fingers over the gold-leaf lettering of my name on the outside. My mother had given the book to me for Christmas. Maybe she thought writing things down in it would help. But it didn't if the maids were reading it. Tears stung my eyes. "What's the matter, darlin'? Sure there's no need to cry." I pushed the diary under my pillow. It wasn't safe there, either. It wasn't safe anywhere.

I took my brush off the dresser and tugged it through my hair, watching the blur of myself in the mirror, tugging and tugging. And those awful maids spreading the story that Miss Müller's father was a Nazi. As if everyone wasn't against her enough, me included. My brushstrokes got slower and slower. The silence of the dorm pressed against my ears. Of course if her father *had* been a Nazi, and she really had a picture to prove it, then the idea of her being a spy was even easier to believe. My heart began pumping and the milk of magnesia taste was mysteriously back in my throat. Should I go and look for myself? Should I?

I peeked around the door of my cubie. No one was there, and all I could hear was the normal sound of the lavatory running in the bathroom. It was the one in the third stall, the one that had no seat, the one that gurgled day and night. Not another noise anywhere. I'd never have a chance like this again.

As I tiptoed up the corridor, I thought, sneak, sneak. Peek, peek. But then I thought, there's a war on. My cousin Bryan's fighting in France. Last night Belfast was bombed.

Here was the door to Miss Müller's room. I'd been this far before, but never inside. We weren't allowed in teachers' rooms, for some unexplained reason.

"In case of hanky-panky," Ada explained.

"What's hanky-panky?"

"Oh, you know," Ada said grandly, the way she did when she was pretending to be smarter than us, but she wasn't really.

It must be the same kind of reason Hillary's mum doesn't want her alone in a train carriage with a man, I thought vaguely. Well, not the same, but something for parents to worry about.

I turned the knob. The door opened.

Miss Müller's bed wasn't made. Girls had to make their own in the mornings, but the maids did the teachers'. The maids obviously hadn't come to this dorm yet.

On Miss Müller's dresser was the picture of her and

her mother. I'd seen it lots of times in plain sight when I came to her door. Sarah Neely had told Hillary the other one was behind it.

I went quickly across the cubicle and picked up the wooden frame.

In the distance I heard talking. The maids were heading this way, free to do whatever they wanted to do. I could hear the swish, swish as they dry mopped the corridor.

Quick, quick, Jessie.

There was something behind the first picture. That much of Hillary's story was true. My fingers poked at it, got hold of the edge. A German soldier stared out at me from the second photograph. His uniform had a high collar and pouchy trousers, and he wore knee-high black boots. I knew what that uniform was. We booed soldiers wearing it when we saw them on the Pathé newsreels, goose-stepping in line, holding their arms up stiff in the Nazi salute. I looked closely at the picture. There was a swastika on a band around the soldier's arm.

I swallowed down the sour magnesia taste and turned the photo over. The back was covered with spidery writing in German, but Miss Müller was a good teacher and I could read what it said. "To my dear daughter Daphne. Honor the Fatherland. August 1938."

The maids had come as far as Maureen's room now. The young-sounding one, who was probably Sarah with the pimples, was saying, "She's still at the knitting. And would you look at all the dropped stitches! It'll be a lucky fellow that gets *this* balaclava."

They were hooting and laughing. Probably they laughed like this over my diary. I wished I could stick

61

their heads in their buckets of soapy water till they blubbered for mercy.

My fingers were shaking so much, it was hard to slide the picture back behind the other one and set the frame on the dresser.

The maids were going into Lizzie Mag's room. Bridget, the older, gravelly-voiced one, was talking. "Now here's a wee girl I'm sorry for. That last letter from her ma was terrible altogether."

I stood, turned to stone. Now was my chance to get away without being seen, but I couldn't move. They'd read Lizard's letters. How could they? Lizzie Mag was so private with her letters. She never shared them the way the rest of us did, standing in a huddle, reading them out loud. Mummy knew not to mention Daddy's problem when she wrote to me. All the dorm would know if she did.

Lizzie Mag whispered to me once why she didn't share hers. "They're too sad, Jess. I cry when I read them. They need to be only for me."

I hugged her. I understood.

Now the maids knew. I bet they didn't cry. There was no way to have a secret in Alveara.

Sarah was talking again in a tired, superior voice. "It makes you thankful to have a regular ma and da, so it does."

"Pass me that Mansion polish, Sarah girl," Bridget ordered, and gave a great sigh. "The mother angry all the time about the father leaving her and going off with that . . . what did she call her, Sarah?"

"I forget. But it's a young girl, anyway. And then him writing to this sweet thing here and telling her he's leaving the ma, but he isn't leaving *her*. That she's his own darlin' daughter. Ach sure, he would say that. Telling her he'll be back for her as soon as the war's over."

Bridget gave another sigh. "Mark my words, it'll be a tug-of-war and her in the middle. Give that mirror a wee skite of a wipe," she ordered Sarah.

I could hear the squeaking of the duster across the glass. Sarah was warbling an old ballad at the top of her voice: "There's a spot in me heart that no colleen may own."

Silently I opened Miss Müller's door and tiptoed away. Neither of the maids saw me.

8

I RAN ACROSS the quad to assembly hall, jumping the puddles and drifts of wet, slippery leaves. The rain had stopped but the oak trees dripped showers of ice water, catching me just as I ran beneath them. My blouse was wetter than the other one had been. I didn't care. Too many thoughts jumbled in my head. That picture! I still couldn't believe it.

In the corner closest to the gym, eight members of the Officer Training Corps in their khaki uniforms were marching. The voice of Mr. Guy, the OTC officer, carried across to me. Mr. Guy was particularly handsome in his OTC uniform. Everyone in uniform looked handsome, Maureen had said, and then paused. "Well, not everyone. Someone small and round like Mr. Bolton shouldn't join up. He's not the right shape."

"We'll tell him," Ada had said. "He'll probably be glad for the advice."

But Mr. Guy looked like a film star in his uniform— Tyrone Power, maybe.

"Right turn. Atten . . . tion!" he called.

Usually there were about twenty sixth-form boys out for morning drill, but this was no ordinary day. I was sur-

prised there were any, since we were an hour behind ourselves this morning. The quad clock said ten minutes to
ten instead of ten minutes to nine, the way it did during
assembly on other mornings. But in another way I was surprised there weren't more, after last night. If I were a boy,
I'd have been begging to be in the OTC preparing to go
fight the Germans. All these sixth formers would graduate
in June, and then they could enlist in the British army.

"It's not fair to girls," Ada had said, and we agreed.
But nobody listened to us.

Inside assembly they were singing the closing hymn.
Darn! I shouldn't have talked so long to Nursie, otherwise I might have made it.

"Lord dismiss us with thy blessing," drifted out
through the doors, along with the squeak of violins from
the school orchestra. It would be as much as my life was
worth to try sneaking in there now. I slowed down.

Greta Ludowski was sitting on the wide steps, one of
her books underneath her to keep her bottom off the wet
bricks. I slowed even more, went up a couple of steps,
and leaned on the railing beside her.

Actually, I didn't want to have to talk to her, or even
stand next to her, but it would have looked funny if I
didn't, since we were the only two there. I had things to
think about and sort out in my head. How would I face
Miss Müller now that I knew about her father? I'd be able
to think as much as I wanted, though, because Greta
wouldn't talk much. She hardly ever did. The trouble was,
even being in her company made me uncomfortable.

Greta had come to Alveara last year. The night before
she was to arrive, Old Rose had called us into her sitting
room. To be called into Old Rose's sitting room was the

scariest thing in the world and we were biting our nails, wondering what we'd done. Mean Jean was holding hard to her silver crucifix, and lots of us were doing the Catholic business of crossing ourselves and rolling our eyes heavenward for help and consolation. When we found out Old Rose just wanted to tell us about a new girl, we crossed ourselves again with the relief of it all. She told us about Greta in her best Shakespearean voice.

"This poor girl has been through such dreadful experiences," Old Rose said. "After her parents got her out of Poland, she was sent by circuitous routes to live with an elderly aunt in County Antrim. The aunt, a Mrs. Wachpool, asked the school governors to make an exception in Greta's case and allow her to board here. As you probably know, we have never had a Jewish student before. Because of her religion Greta will always be excused from prayers and from assembly," Old Rose concluded—which was why Greta was sitting outside on the steps now, of course.

"Did her parents get out of Poland, too, Miss Rose?" Lizzie Mag had asked in a frightened little voice.

Old Rose had spread her hands. "As far as anyone knows they're still there. Which bodes no good. Being Jewish is perilous wherever the Nazis are in power."

We'd sat quietly, thinking about Greta who was to come and her terrible situation.

"Do you think maybe they were killed, Miss Rose?" That was Mean Jean Ross, her hushed whisper reminding us all of the worst possibility. Mean Jean loved to come up with the worst possibility.

Old Rose lowered her voice. "That is conceivable. But we must never, never intimate to Greta that we suspect such a contingency."

We'd talked about it in the dorm afterward, sitting on my bed, vowing to be friendly as could be with Greta. She was to be in Sleeping Beauty dorm, but we'd still see her in Long Parlor and the Common Room. We might even have her in some of our classes.

"And we'll never never imitate that we suspect . . ." Maureen began in a chilling, mournful voice.

"It's intimate, intimate," Ada said, irritated. "Honestly! Can't you ever get anything right, Mo?"

"Intimate." Maureen pursed her mouth and crinkled up her Arcs de Triomphe. "Wait a second. . . . I thought intimate meant like . . . you know . . . with a boy."

"Heaven save us." Ada had flopped back on the bed.

But we promised one another that we'd be careful with Greta, and loving and understanding, too. We'd listen and console.

"It will be like part of our war effort," Maureen said.

The trouble was, Greta didn't want our love and understanding. She didn't want to tell us anything about her ordeal or get our opinions or even say bad things about the Germans. She kept to herself, moving silently, staring into the distance. At first we thought maybe she didn't know English very well, and we spoke slowly and loudly to her. "Greta—would—you—like—to—play—rounders—with—us—on—the—lawn?" We stopped that way of talking when we found out she used better English than most of us—definitely better than Maureen, as Ada said.

"She wants to be left alone," Lizzie Mag told us. "She's hurting too much."

"Suffering from emotional disturbance" was the way Old Rose put it.

And no wonder. Two mornings a week Greta saw a

psychiatrist, the word always whispered among us behind our hands. After we found out, we pretty much stayed away from her.

Once when we went for a ramble by the river, Lizzie Mag asked Greta to be her walk partner. I was really hurt and mad, too, because Lizard and I were always partners in the crocodile when we walked two by two in a long, winding line. I ended up having to walk with Marion Kelleher, who was a swot, studying day and night. She spent the whole ramble telling me why Pythagoras was a genius and how numbers became for him the ultimate way to interpret the universe. As if I cared.

But I couldn't ever stay mad at Lizzie Mag for long. When we were friends again, she told me Greta hadn't said one word during the whole ramble. Lizzie Mag talked to her every time she saw her, though, even after the rest of us had given up trying. Lizard was always nice to everyone. I thought of her inside assembly now, saving a seat for me, defending Mean Jean Ross if Maureen and Ada were saying bad stuff about her.

Lizzie Mag defended everyone. It wasn't fair about her parents. How could they have a tug-of-war with poor little Lizard in between them? Bad enough having them so far away in India, but now this.

I glanced sideways at Greta sitting on her schoolbook, staring across the wet quad. What was she thinking? About her parents? Poland? What? It was so sad for her, all of it.

I gave a little cough to remind her I was there and said conversationally, "Well, I hope we won't have any more air raids." Lizzie Mag would have been proud of me.

I wasn't expecting an answer, and I was startled when Greta said casually: "The Germans like to bomb."

I nodded. I'd seen her in the shelter and I'd known she wasn't too impressed with our air raid.

Inside assembly hall they were now into another verse of the closing hymn. The cello was way off key, sounding like a seal barking. "Thanks for mercies past received," the Alveara students sang with gusto.

Greta might be wondering what mercies she'd received. Well, she *did* get out of Poland. I was pleased that she'd said something to me. It was a kind of crack in her armor and probably a good sign. It would also be something else to tell the girls in the dorm later. Way down the list, after my other discoveries of the day. But maybe the air raid had brought Greta closer to us. After all, we all hated the Germans, and last night the war had come to our city, too.

"Listen." I leaned toward her trying to open up the crack a little more. "We have reason to think Miss Müller might be a German spy."

Greta turned her face toward me. Looking into her eyes was like looking into deep, still water. The depths made me nervous.

I shifted my gaze and stared across the quad.

"Squad . . . halt!" Mr. Guy bellowed, and I had a mysterious flash of a German school somewhere, a quad like this one. Linden trees maybe, German sixth formers training to fight us. Like a game, like checkers. Your move, my move. You bomb, we bomb. I shook my head. What a traitorous thought.

"You think she might be a *spy*?" Greta repeated. "Why?"

"She goes spy walking on the roof at night," I said, "and we're going to find out more. Ada and Maureen and Lizzie Mag and I are planning to follow her when she leaves her room."

Greta didn't speak. She watched me carefully.

It was a funny thing that I'd noticed before. When a person doesn't say anything, just waits, the other person has to jump in to fill the silence gap. It must be a law of physics, Pythagoras, or something like that. Silence is not always golden—sometimes it's creepy. "Miss Müller's father was a Nazi," I added. "I saw his picture."

"Most Germans are." Greta's lips twisted. Was she laughing at me? There was something in her voice that made me think so. She talked the way some teachers talked to the little kindergartners.

"And if we do find out she is a spy . . ." I said, menacingly.

"Yes? Then what will you do?"

I was wishing I hadn't started this. It suddenly sounded so fake, like a story out of the *Girls' Crystal*, not real in the way Greta knew reality.

"Well, we'll tell Old Rose . . . or the police."

"Will you kill her?"

"*Kill* her?" I gave a high little laugh. "Of course we won't kill her. I mean—"

"When you follow Miss Müller, can I come with you?" Greta asked, her voice so urgent that it made me instinctively slide down the steps farther away from her.

"Well . . ." Oh, why, *why* had I brought this up? "You see it's really the whole dorm, Snow White dorm, not just me . . ." I stammered. "It's not my decision, and we don't know exactly when—"

"You can come and get me. I waken very easily. I know how to be quiet."

"Yes, but—"

"They killed my father." Greta's face never changed expression.

"Pardon?" I said, though I had heard perfectly well. Too well.

I pressed myself backward so hard against the railing that I felt it cut into my back. Oh no! Oh cripes! "You mean the Germans?" I asked. Goofy question. My stomach was starting to stab in that familiar way that shouts "Cramps coming." The milk of magnesia wasn't strong enough to handle this. "How do you know they killed him? I thought you didn't know."

"We have ways of finding out." Greta stood up. "His name was on the last list that was smuggled through." The textbook lay open, the pages crumpled where she'd sat. A robin zoomed down from a branch, grabbed a worm, and zoomed back into the tree. From assembly hall I heard the babble of voices, the scraping of feet. Assembly was over.

"I have to come with you when you follow her," Greta said. She was holding my shoulder the way I'd held little Hillary's girdle at dispensary.

"All right," I said, but I didn't mean it. Greta let go and I gave myself a shake. Lying was not something I did except maybe in a very big emergency. This was a very big emergency. When we followed Miss Müller, we definitely were not, *not* going to take Greta Ludowski with us. Goodness alone knew what *she'd* do!

9

THE TEACHERS WERE coming out of Assembly Hall, Old Rose sweeping along in front like Cleopatra, Queen of the Nile, Mr. Atkinson behind her, his head tilted back on his skinny neck, his sharp nose poking in every direction. Miss Müller walked next to Mr. Bolton. He seemed to be her friend. Did the rest of the teachers like her, or did they hiss at her too, among themselves?

Beside me I felt Greta tense, and she muttered something I didn't understand. Maybe it was Polish. I wished with all my heart that the world was the way it used to be when I'd never heard of Nazis, when Greta was safe in Poland with her parents, and Miss Müller was back in Germany. A time when Alveara was just a school, not great but okay. When nobody dreamed that bombs would fall on Belfast. And oh, how I wished that I hadn't blabbed to Greta today. She was on the track now . . . not the way we were, but in a more deadly way that frightened me. "Will you kill her?" she'd asked. *Kill her*.

Swarms of girls came pouring out of assembly. Lizzie Mag rushed toward me. "Lots of girls are leaving Alveara," she said. "Their parents are taking them home because Belfast is too dangerous. Betty Austin's going and Selina Brown."

I looked at Lizard, her blond hair straight after the failure of last night's curls, the rest of her so pale and neat. And I wished another wish, that she could be in India with her parents and that they loved each other and loved her. "You're wishing your life away, Jess," my mother always said in a sad sort of way.

"No, Mummy, just wishing some lives could be better," I'd answer.

"Helen Payne's gone already," Lizard went on. "Old Boots took her trunk."

"Was that the sensation?" I asked.

"No. There was more. Things about Pearl Carson and Michael Moran. It's awful. Wait till you hear...." She stopped. "What's the matter, Jess? You look so ... so jumpy. Was Nursie awful?"

Before I could answer, someone touched my arm. "Come for me," Greta said.

I nodded.

Lizzie Mag stared. "She's talking to you? Come for her where?"

"I'll tell you later," I whispered.

Ada and Maureen had arrived on my other side. "Have you told her yet about Pearl Carson?" Maureen whispered. "It was too funny."

"What?" I said.

"It wasn't funny at all," Lizzie Mag said.

"Old Rose gave us a lecture as long as Paddy's leg about our disgraceful shenanigans last night." Maureen giggled and tossed her hair. "And then she glared blazes right at Pearl Carson and said, 'One girl in particular dishonored the school by her offensive behavior with a boy. Disciplinary action will be taken. We are seriously considering expulsion.' "

Maureen could do a great takeoff on Old Rose's haughty voice.

"Expulsion!" We'd never had anybody expelled. Pearl's behavior must have been *really* offensive. "Do you think she will be expelled?" I breathed. "And what about the boy she was with? What disciplinary action is going to be taken against him?"

"Oh, none probably. It was Michael Moran. Head boy, captain of the cricket team." Ada waved her fingers airily. "Nothing disgraceful shall touch the head boy."

"Speaking of boys, here they come." Maureen wet her finger and stroked under her lashes, which gave them a shiny, glistening effect till the hairs dried.

"Move along, move along, girls." Miss Gaynor pressed on our shoulders to remove us quickly from the boys' contaminating presence. I looked back and saw Ian with Curly Pritchard. Ian was wearing his navy-blue V-neck regulation sweater. I loved it when he wore that instead of his blazer. I could see him better, or at least more of him.

Ian smiled at me and nodded, and a lock of his straight blond hair fell over his forehead. Oh, gee willikers! Had those nice masculine lips of his really pressed against mine last night? That seemed so far away. Too bad. The good things had gotten lost in all the horrible things that were happening. Tonight, though, I would write about him in my diary and . . . I stopped. No, not in my diary. What if the maids should read it?

We were crowding forward, sheep being nuzzled by the sheepdog that was Miss Gaynor.

"We're to go directly from our lockers to second-period class," Lizzie Mag told me.

"Wait a second," I said. She and Ada and Maureen slowed. There'd be no way to talk at our lockers, where Miss Hardcastle would be on sheepdog duty, nipping at us to hurry and get to class, and then at lunch we would be in our assigned seats with eavesdroppers all around. I spoke quickly. "Miss Müller's father was a Nazi soldier, and I think she went up on the roof in March, the night the munitions blew up."

The three of them were staring at me as if I'd gone mad. "A Nazi soldier?" Ada mouthed. "Munitions?"

"Come to my room for a meeting, right after school," I said.

"We have tennis," Lizard reminded me.

"It'll be canceled. It's going to rain again." I looked up at the sky, where clouds piled and jumbled, gray as geese. A few big raindrops fell, spotting the quad.

Miss Gaynor was heading toward us again, impatiently waving us forward.

"Miss Gaynor," Ada said, "I have to tell Jessie about the phone calls home. She doesn't know."

"What phone calls?" I asked.

"Well, don't take all day over it, Ada Sinclair," Miss Gaynor said.

"No, Miss Gaynor." Ada made a face at her departing back. "We're all to take turns calling home today from Old Rose's sitting room," Ada said. "They've posted the times on the assembly door. You're three twenty, Jess.

I'm three fifteen, right in front of you. They're so generous, giving us five minutes," she said sarcastically.

"Only Lizzie Mag and Greta don't have to call," she added. "You can't call India or Poland." I nodded.

We rushed to our lockers, got our books, and banged the lockers closed again. The corridors were a muddle of girls' bodies and girls' voices. I automatically headed across to bungalow one for my first period, math, and stopped. This was second period, German, with Miss Müller.

I saw Dolly McConnell up ahead on the path. She has German too, so we always walk to class together. "Why do we take German anyway?" Dolly asked me. "It's a fearful waste of time. After we win the war, German will never be spoken again on the face of the earth."

We'd had this conversation before, going down this same winding path.

I shrugged. "My daddy says there are wonderful German poets and writers and musicians. He says I should know about them. That's why, for me."

"My parents say it's the language of commerce, that's why for me." Dolly arranged her lips carefully again, the way she did each time she spoke. Dolly was the only girl in Alveara with wires on her teeth. They were supposed to straighten her bite, whatever that meant. She said she had them only because her dentist was very "avant-garde," whatever that meant also. Poor Dolly! Thank heavens my dentist was just ordinary.

Miss Müller hadn't arrived when we got to the room. The map of Deutschland that used to hang on the wall had been rolled up and stored a couple of months back when someone drew Hitler's face on it, his mustache covering the whole of Westphalia. On the blackboard, still faintly visible though it had been erased a fortnight or so ago, were the outlines of the chalked words TO HELL WITH HITLER. Mr. Atkinson had lectured all Miss Müller's students very severely about defacing school property. In future, he said, such monkey business would be punished.

There'd been talk just after the war started of discontinuing German at Alveara, but the board of governors said academia must always rise above politics, and besides after the war there would be a need for German speakers to assist with Germany's reconstruction. Uh-uh, we decided. We were never going to reconstruct that old country. Let it perish.

So here we were, sixteen of us, in German II.

Dolly and I sat together in one of the front rows with the other girls. The boys were spread out in back.

Behind us Pat Crow was telling how she'd seen what Pearl Carson and Michael Moran were doing last night in the shelter, and it was no wonder Pearl had gotten into trouble. Dolly and I turned, all agog. "What? What?"

"You know!" Pat said smugly. She sounded just like Ada, very advanced in forbidden knowledge.

"No, we don't know. That's why we're asking," I said.

Dolly unbared her wired upper teeth to announce, "I know. If they were doing *that*, I know about it. I saw a fearful drawing."

"A drawing of Pearl and Michael Moran?" I asked.

"Of course not. Don't be so silly," Pat said. "Who'd be drawing them?"

Just then Miss Müller came into the classroom. "Guten Morgen, Kinder."

We stood politely. "Guten Morgen, Fräulein Müller."

I could hardly bear to look at her. Honor the Fatherland, her father had commanded. He died, she'd told me. I miss him so much, she'd said. I am so fortunate to work here. You bet you are, I thought.

She gestured to us to sit, but she stood behind her desk. "Öffnet eure Bücher," she said, which meant to open our books. There was a rustle of pages turning.

Suddenly I heard this funny little tinkling noise on the floor. We squirmed and craned our necks to look down. Two small silver beads rolled past along the floor. One hit Miss Müller's shoe, the other bounced off the leg of her desk and stopped. She bent and picked them up.

"Hat jemand diese verloren?" she asked, which meant "Did somebody lose these?"

No one answered, so she set them on her desk.

"Huete Morgen . . ." Miss Müller began. She stopped. Three or four more of the silver beads were rolling merrily around her feet.

"Ball bearings," Dolly whispered to me. "Some of the boys must have brought them."

"Wer macht das?" Miss Müller asked. Her voice had a tremble in it. She was asking who was doing this.

Again no one answered. The boys were all bent over their desks, intent on their German literature books. But someone's hand had to be down, hidden behind the legs in front. The ball bearings kept rolling past us, four, six, ten, some hitting Miss Müller's feet, some going as far as the wall and bouncing back. The room was filled with their silvery noise.

"Hört auf, bitte," Miss Müller said. "Wir müssen mit dem Unterricht weitermachen."

"What did she say?" Dolly whispered.

"We have to get on with the lesson."

The little beads were all over the floor now. The boys had premeditated this, as they say in mystery books.

Miss Müller stood straight. Her face had two red blotches high on the cheekbones, and her hands clutched the edges of her desk as if to keep from falling.

"Heute Morgen studieren wir das berühmte Gedicht 'Die Lorelei' von Heinrich Heine," she said, not loudly enough to have been heard from behind a newspaper.

"Please, Miss Müller, will you translate?"

"This morning we are going to study the famous poem 'Die Lorelei' of Heinrich Heine," she said. Through the flutter of a few turning pages came the uninterrupted rumble of the tiny ball bearings. The floor was covered with them, like confetti on the floor after a wedding.

" 'Ich weiss nicht, was soll es bedeuten,' " Miss Müller read.

Roll, tinkle, rattle. Some of the little balls stopped close to us, and when they did we gave them another nudge with our feet, sending them rolling again. Miss Müller kept on reading. When she finished, she told us more about the beautiful maiden known as the Lorelei, and about the rock that rose so high above the Rhine River, and about how the maiden enticed sailors to their deaths.

A boy's hand went up.

"Ja?"

"Is the rock still there, Miss Müller?"

"Yes, David. It is a piece of history."

"I thought maybe now the Royal Air Force had blasted

79

it out of the Rhine River," David said. "Boom. Boom."
He made plane-diving swoops with his hands.

There was a gust of laughter and some clapping. Then
another flurry of rolling ball bearings.

"We will finish reading the poem," Miss Müller said.

Even through the constant metallic rattle I could recognize the beauty of "Die Lorelei," and I thought, If I live
to be a hundred and the world is at peace, I will never
hear this poem without hearing also the small rumble,
tumble of the ball bearings around Miss Müller's feet.

I would have felt sorry for her if she hadn't been a
Nazi.

10

I GOT EXCUSED from the last ten minutes of last period, chemistry with Stinky Larrimer, so that I could call home. We were doing experiments with Bunsen burners and liquids that turned into gases with disgusting smells. The boys said they loved it, even though they were choking and coughing like the rest of us. I was happy to get away.

There were only two phones in Alveara, one in Mr. Atkinson's study, the other in Old Rose's sitting room. Our parents could ring us and leave messages or arrange for us to ring back. When we did, Old Rose was always right there, sitting by her fire, not listening to our conversations, of course. She'd never do that.

"Talk about censorship," Ada said.

"It's one way to make sure we don't complain," I said. "But you'd think today, after the air raid, she'd have the decency to let us talk to our parents in private." Never. The word *privacy* wasn't in Old Rose's vocabulary. Hers or the maids'.

From outside her sitting room I could faintly hear Ada's voice talking on the phone. In a few seconds she came out and whispered, "Oh yes indeed, Mummy and

Daddy. Miss Rose is being wonderfully kind to us. Everyone is. Oh yes. We were so well organized for air-raid drill there was no panic at all."

Ada pulled down on the corners of her eyes and up on the corners of her lips to make a gargoyle of her face. It was hard not to giggle. Ada looks enough like a gargoyle without exaggerating it. "I could boke," she said, leaning over and making boking noises.

I tap-tapped on the sitting-room door and was sweetly invited to come in. As usual Old Rose was in an armchair close to her nice cozy fire, and the room had that warm, peaty smell that reminded me of home. The *Belfast Newsletter* was open across her knees, and her academic gown was folded over a footstool beside her. When it was off you could plainly see that Old Rose was shaped like an overstuffed sausage. Her legs were thin, though, and when she wore the gown she was well camouflaged.

She turned a fake-concerned face toward me. "Come in, precious. I hope you're not too nervous after last night."

"Not really, Miss Rose." I thought about Ian McManus. His lips had been so warm, and up close there'd been a pepperminty smell, toothpaste maybe. The ads for a certain brand said, "Did you McClean your teeth today?" I tried not to think about Ian because we had a firm belief that Old Rose could read your thoughts by looking at your face, so in her presence it was best to stay blank. She was looking at me closely now.

"Help yourself to the telephone, macushla." Her hand waved toward where it sat on its table in the bay of the mullioned window.

"Thank you, Miss Rose."

"Just sign the book like a good girl."

We had to sign for everything in this place. I put my name under Ada's. Now our parents and the parents of all the names in front of mine and after could be billed for the calls.

"And please keep your conversation short, Jessica. We have a lot of concerned parents today who want to talk to their daughters."

"Yes, Miss Rose."

"I did speak with your parents earlier. They called very early indeed and I was able to reassure them." Her voice let me know she felt it was really thoughtless of them to have disturbed her like that. Then she smiled again. "Of course they want reassurance from yourself."

I nodded and dialed home, hearing the ring, visualizing the phone on the hall stand. My father's squashed cap would be hanging on the rack, the umbrellas and walking sticks would be standing higgledy-piggledy in their brass holder, the stained-glass window in the hall door would be dropping its red and green patterns on the wallpaper. I swallowed down a rush of homesickness. Just thinking of home could do that to me.

Mummy would be getting up from the fire now, complaining a bit if Daddy was there. "I don't know why we have to keep the phone in the drafty hall anyway. It would be far better in here."

They'd been having this argument as long as I could remember. The phone couldn't be changed because of something to do with the plug.

Daddy would have the radio on. He had to listen to the prices of pigs and potatoes and grass seed, though he

83

wasn't a farmer himself. He'd likely be listening . . . if he was there.

Someone picked up the phone. "Mummy?"

"Jess?" My mother's voice was warm, filled with worry. "Are you all right, love?"

"I am. The bombs weren't anywhere near us."

"I know. Old Rose told us that this morning. Oh, Jessie, we were that bothered. We heard the German planes go over last night. The whole town was out in Bank Square looking up at the sky. Your daddy got into the car and we started off to go and get you, but the police stopped everybody on the edge of Belfast. They had roadblocks up. No one was to be let in or out of the city except emergency vehicles." She stopped for breath.

"We were fine," I said. "I'm sorry you were so worried."

Old Rose had the *Belfast Newsletter* up in front to her face, reading supposedly, but the page was too quiet. I saw the big, black headline, "German Bombs Rock Belfast." Below was a picture of houses and fire engines and people running about. There wasn't the littlest rustle of the paper. I knew Old Rose was listening to me with those big antenna ears of hers. Let me utter one wrong word and she'd pounce.

"Now, Jess," my mum was saying, "if you want to come home and be out of Belfast in case of another raid, we'll come for you. We have enough petrol."

She and I stood, me here, her there, the two of us listening to each other's thoughts. All the reasons I'd been sent to Alveara in the first place hummed in the space between us. There was no school near Ballylo, and enough money was coming in from the family business and something called "investments" so they could send me away to a good school.

Besides, if I were there I'd be with my father ... my father who drank himself senseless every day of the week, who had to be carried from the pub night after night. Somebody was always banging our front-door knocker. "Here's the boss, missus. He's had a drop too much. I'm bringin' him home for you."

And the click of my mother's purse opening, a half crown changing hands. "Thanks, Paddy. Very good of you."

"Will you be needing help to get him up the stairs and into bed, missus?"

"No, thank you. I can manage." My father limp and boneless as a scarecrow, but still gentle and loving even when he didn't know who he was or where he was.

Maybe the same scenes were flashing along the telephone wires between my mother and me, the same remembered heartbreaking words.

"Your grandma and grandpa think we should bring you back right away," my mother was saying. "But ..." Her voice got fainter. "But perhaps you're better staying where you are."

"Yes. I'm fine here."

Old Rose gave me a dazzling, false-toothed smile around the edge of the newspaper and said in a stage whisper, "One minute left, Jessie dear."

I quickly asked about my cousin Bryan.

"Aunt Clara hasn't had a letter in a long time. She's awfully worried."

And then I heard Mummy say, "No, Magnus. You don't need to talk to her at all." And the dry slide of the phone being dragged across the hall table and silence, then the boom of my father's voice, slurred and thick. "Jessie, Jessie me darlin'?"

"Daddy?"

Old Rose's newspaper gave a little twitch. Did she know? I always wondered if she knew. I turned my back and stared out the windows at the Alveara grounds, the roll of wet lawns, the dripping trees, the darkened purples of the rhododendrons that lined the drive. Rain slanted down, thin as threads.

"I'll not have them dropping bombs on my daughter," my father bellowed. "Do you hear me, you murdering Huns? Stay away from my girl."

I didn't know if the murdering Huns could hear him, but surely Old Rose could. I held the phone tight against my ear and tried to curve my arm around it. Mummy and he were having words now. There were the sounds of her trying to get the phone away from him.

Then her voice. "Jess?"

"I have to go," I said. "I love you. Tell Daddy I love him, too."

"Hang up now, Jessie." That was Old Rose using her most imperious tone. "We mustn't take more time than we're entitled to. We must abide by the rules."

Old yap!

I hung up.

A turf shifted in the grate, sending a firework display of orange sparks up the chimney. At either side of the hearth Old Rose had a white china dog; their names were Gog and Magog.

"How is your father?" she asked me, sitting forward.

"He has good days and bad days," I lied. He had only

bad days. Good hours and bad hours would have been more like it.

Old Rose's little green eyes watched me carefully.

"What do the doctors say about his illness, Jessie? Will he get over it?" Once I'd hinted he had rheumatism, but I was always vague.

"It's hard to say," I said, and backed toward the door. We always backed away from Miss Rose's presence, the way commoners do leaving the presence of a queen. Ada said it was because we were afraid of getting a knife in the back.

"Thank you for letting me use the telephone," I said.

She nodded graciously.

What if I stopped right now and said, "Did you know Miss Müller's likely a German spy, and Greta Ludowski has a thought of killing her?" That would get Old Rose out of her chair in a hurry. That would take her mind off my father. I backed myself so fast, I bumped into the door.

Pat Crow was waiting her turn to go in. "Is she there?" she asked.

"Is water wet?" I asked. "She's crouched like an octopus with an ear at the end of each arm."

I stood there in the hall for a moment, looking up at the portrait of Miss Helen Maguire, headmistress of Alveara 1911 to 1924. My chest hurt. Miss Maguire wore a dark dress with a high banded collar, almost like the one on the Nazi uniform, except that Miss Maguire had a cameo brooch pinned on the front of hers. Her face danced and dazzled through the blur in my eyes. My mother had a cameo.

My father had a medal he got in World War I when he

fought in the North Irish Horse Regiment. He also had a piece of shrapnel in the palm of his right hand, so his hand didn't open all the way. I guess the doctors at the front couldn't get the shrapnel out. "They poked at it plenty," Daddy told me. "I think the one who worked on me was a dentist." His palm curved in a way that just fit the back of my neck when he was telling me, "I do love you, darlin'. I'm going to do better. I'm taking the pledge, so I am."

I pressed my face to the wall, found my hanky in the pocket of my tunic, and blew my nose. At least he was alive, I told myself, not like Greta's father. And he wasn't any worse; it was just . . . you forgot how bad he was when you didn't see him every day. You forgot.

11

WHEN I LIFTED my head, I saw Miss Müller coming in the front door. Her long, beige raincoat was dark with wet and she had on the funny little rubber overshoes she wore instead of Wellingtons. Somehow she always looked romantic and foreign. Anyone could tell she wasn't ordinary Irish. Miss Müller was carrying one of the small white paper bags from the College Chemists that was just outside the Alveara gate. Not that we had gates anymore. The gates and railings had been taken away to be melted into bullets.

Miss Müller smiled a timid kind of smile. "Hello, Jessie."

"Hello." I gave my nose a last feeble blow and put my hanky in my tunic pocket.

Her face became sad. "You were calling your parents? They were worried, I'm sure."

"Yes, very."

I had to pass her if I wanted to go back to the dorm, which I did want to. No use trying to go back to class— last bell would be going any second. Normally, before the war, I would have been thrilled to have Miss Müller talk with me, maybe even walk along the corridor beside me. There was a sort of fairy-tale air about her. But now I just wanted to get away.

I hurried along as if I had a very important appointment.

"Jessie." Her voice stopped me. "May I speak with you?"

"Me? Now?"

"Yes. Please wait. If you are going back to the dorm, I will come with you."

"Well, I was . . ." Where else could I be going? "All right," I muttered in a grudging, surly voice, and I stood miserably while she sat on the carved hall bench and took off her overshoes.

"There." She shook water from them and glanced down at the College Chemists bag. "I walked down to get some aspirin," she said, as if I needed an explanation of where she'd been. I needed an explanation of where she'd been last night, not now.

"You seem to buy a lot of aspirin," I said.

"I have headaches," she said.

"Maybe you don't get enough sleep," I said. I was astonished that I was talking this way to a teacher. I reminded myself that she wasn't a teacher, she was a German. I didn't look at her as she began to walk beside me.

"You're right," she said. "I don't sleep well at all."

We took a few more silent steps. Then she touched my arm and said again, "Jessie." She stopped and I had to stop too. Her dark hair curled against the paleness of her face. The rain had brought out the faint smell of apricots, the way the smell of a honeysuckle hedge is sweeter after a summer shower.

"You were in my German class today," she said. "You saw what happened with . . . with . . ."

Sometimes still Miss Müller had trouble with an English word. We used to think it was very attractive and we'd try forgetting a word ourselves, looking puzzled the way she did. On us it just looked dumb. I supplied the word for her now. "I saw what happened with the ball bearings."

She nodded. "Also in the dining room, there was that hissing." She bit her lip.

"Yes."

Her fingers folded the paper bag at the top, unfolded it, folded again. "It is hard for me," she said. "I understand why, but it is still hard."

Nancy Eden and Dolly McConnell came walking along the corridor toward us carrying their violin cases. They'd be on their way back from orchestra practice early. They gave us inquisitive looks as they passed, and Dolly bared her teeth wires in a semi-smile and said, "Guten Tag, Miss Müller."

"Guten Tag," Miss Müller replied.

I was wishing they hadn't seen me standing there talking to her. German lover, they'd think. Probably say it, too. I'd tell them she stuck to me like adhesive tape.

"Does it make you uncomfortable to be seen with me?" Miss Müller asked gently. "I'm sorry."

"It's all right," I muttered, though it wasn't.

"I wanted to ask you a favor, Jessie."

Oh cheese! A favor from me. I edged back till I felt the safety of the corridor wall behind me.

"I have always considered you my friend," Miss Müller said, "in spite of . . ." She stopped, but I didn't think it was because she'd lost another English word. In this half-light her eyes were dark blue, almost the navy blue of our uniform.

91

"You know, I can't help being half German. I didn't choose that my two countries should be at war."

Pat Crow was coming out of Old Rose's sitting room now, heading along the corridor toward us in one direction, and Betsy Crawford was rushing and puffing from the other direction. Betsy passed us first. "Crumbs, I'm late," she said. "Old Rose will have a cow. Oh, excuse me, Miss Müller. I didn't realize it was you with Jessie." Betsy Crawford was blind as a beetroot and wouldn't admit to it because she didn't want to wear glasses. She also always had gaps at the top of her stockings. Lizzie Mag said it was because she couldn't see.

"She can *feel*, can't she," Ada asked. It was true. We were always checking for gaps with our fingers, pulling the legs of our knickers down so they met the stocking tops.

Betsy turned in my direction, and her look said "Talking to the enemy," plainer than if she'd spoken.

"Gaps," I said loudly. Her face got red as fire and I was glad.

When she left I said, "I don't know what you think I can do, Miss Müller," speaking faster than fast before Pat Crow got to us in about fifteen seconds.

"You could do a lot. You may not know this, but you're well liked and quite a leader. You could perhaps soften them toward me. Try to explain I'm not against . . ." She stopped as Pat Crow reached us.

Pat ignored Miss Müller entirely. "You know what my dad just told me?" she asked, looking only at me. "One of those houses on the Shore Road got a direct hit last night. The father was coming off the night shift in the shipyard. He's a welder. And he came rushing home after the siren and everything, and when he got there, there was no

92

house, just this big hole in the ground. His wife and two children were inside." Pat lowered her voice. "They could only find bits of them, Jessie. Isn't that awful?"

Miss Müller shifted her little rain boots from one hand to the other and kept her head lowered.

"Even their dog was killed," Pat said. "My daddy said the man went ranting, raving mad. They had to hold him down and they had to get an ambulance and take him to Purdysburn." She glared at Miss Müller. "In case you don't know, Miss Müller, Purdysburn is the hospital for the insane."

"I'm sure the planes didn't mean to drop a bomb on innocent people." Miss Müller's English was suddenly so bad I could hardly understand it.

"The RAF would *never* kill civilians," Pat said coldly. "They're trained not to, and anyway they're too decent."

Miss Müller bit her lip. "Lots of Germans are being killed every day and night. You think your Royal Air Force doesn't drop bombs on us?"

I stared at her, dumbfounded.

"Well," Pat Crow said, "now we know where *you* stand."

Pat stalked off, but my feet seemed glued to the floor. *You? Us?*

"Jessie!" Miss Müller tried to put her hand on my arm again, but I squirmed away. "I was not the one who dropped the bomb," she said.

"We know that. And we know other things, too." The glue had come unstuck, freeing my feet, and I was running toward the dorm. An Alveara girl did not run except in case of fire or hemorrhage. We'd had that pounded into us, but who cared? I passed Pat Crow, who shouted

93

"Jessie" also and tried to catch up. But Pat was as thick as a stump and didn't run too well. Nobody could have caught me. I ran to the dorm, jerked open the door of my cubie, and threw myself on the bed.

I was still there staring up at the ceiling when last bell rang. I heard Miss Müller come into the dorm. I heard her door open. She'd be hanging up her wet raincoat now, putting her overshoes on the high shelf, brushing her wet hair. Then sliding out the picture of her Nazi father, the two of them smiling at each other.

There was noise and shouting as everyone came back from last period. Locker doors slammed, and then Lizzie Mag and Ada and Maureen came clumping into the dorm.

"Jessie, are you here already?" Lizzie Mag tapped on my door, the others behind her. "You were right," she said, beaming. "No tennis. It's raining as usual."

"Look what Ada got," Maureen said, and Ada hefted up a big cardboard box with her name in dark print across the front. "Tuck box . . . from home," she said.

I sat up and brushed my hair away from my face.

"Your eyes are all red and puffy," Maureen accused.

"So?" I asked.

"Did you make your call? Was your daddy bad again?" Lizard asked in her little sympathetic voice.

I nodded. "But there's so much more to tell you." I kept my voice low and pointed at Miss Müller's room.

Ada slid the tuck-box string off and we leaned over the contents. Her mother had sent a barm brack loaf filled with currants and raisins, a jar of Marmite to spread on it, and a sponge cake wrapped in a tea cloth. I got my long metal nail file, sharp as a dagger, that I kept in my dresser

94

drawer, and Ada hacked the barm brack into curranty hunks that we ate as I talked.

I told about slipping into Miss Müller's room earlier.

Lizard gasped. "You'd have been expelled, Jess, if they'd caught you."

I told about the photograph behind the other photograph. But I didn't tell how I'd heard the maids talking about Lizard's letters. I'd never mention that. We discussed everything in low whispers. Then Maureen went to get our tooth mugs and fill them with water, because Marmite always stuck to the tops of our mouths. It was all right if we spread it on bread, but the taste by itself was gummy. Still, the salty, beef-flavored stuff was more delicious than anything else in the world.

Then Lizzie Mag said "Sh!" and put her fingers to her lips, and we listened to Miss Müller's door softly open and close as she left the dorm.

"Probably going to the teachers' lounge to act as nice as pie," Maureen said, and Ada closed her eyes and said dramatically: " 'By the pricking of my thumbs, something wicked this way comes.' "

"Exactly," Maureen agreed.

I told them how Miss Müller had asked me to speak up for her and then how she talked of *them* and *us*. "Well, now we know," I said, repeating Pat Crow's words.

Ada set the sponge cake on the bed and sliced it up. "Why would she think you'd be on her side?" she asked. "What a cheek!"

"Because Jessie is kind," Lizzie Mag said, giving me one of her sweet little smiles.

We ate the cake, the dusting of sugar smudging mustaches over our lips, snow sugar dropping on my quilt.

The raspberry jam inside had dried a bit, but the cake was still wonderful.

"Your mum sends the best boxes," Lizzie Mag said.

"It's because we have the grocer's shop. She can get eggs and butter and sugar to bake with." Ada peered into the Marmite jar. "I have to save half of everything for Jack. Good thing Mummy sends the package to me first. Those boy boarders would gorb it all down." She began wrapping up the rest of the cake.

"My ayah used to make delicious ladoos and samosas," Lizard said, "especially at festival times." She lay back on the bed. "They were always so small and so perfect, filled with meat and spices, and we'd go, my daddy and mummy and I, to the festival. Ayah would come too, and she'd carry me."

Lizard's eyes were half closed as if she were dreaming. "Diwali . . . the festival of lights. Everything's so beautiful. The candles flickering in the dark and the smell of incense. Sometimes my daddy and mummy would dance together, and sometimes he'd dance with me. And he was so tall and so handsome. He'd call me his little princess because that's my name, you see. . . ." She paused.

"Of course. Elizabeth Margaret," I said, and touched her hand, which was covered with sugar. And I thought how strange it was, all of us pretending about our fathers, me, Lizard, Miss Müller. All of us except Greta, and her father was dead. You probably don't have to pretend anymore when your father's dead. I shivered.

"Could I have one more lick of Marmite?" Maureen asked, unaware as usual of the vibrations around her.

Ada said unless Maureen was hit over the head with a cricket bat, she didn't know what was happening.

Maureen was sitting with her finger ready to dip when someone knocked on my door.

"Who is it?" I asked as we fumbled to hide the tuck box. We were supposed to eat treats in Long Parlor, not in our rooms where crumbs could bring mice—and did.

"It's Greta," the voice said.

Maureen raised her eyebrows.

"Come in," I called.

Never before had Greta Ludowski been in my room. Never before had she been in our dorm.

Lizzie Mag moved closer to the cubie wall. "You can sit by me."

Ada hadn't finished wrapping the cake. "Want a piece?" she asked.

"Yes, please," Greta said.

We watched her eat, none of us saying a word till she finished.

She wiped her fingers on the face flannel that I offered her, still damp from this morning. "Thank you." She looked at us, one by one. "So?" she asked. "Tonight we go?"

"That's not the plan," I told her. "Tonight, first, I'm going to listen. If Miss Müller comes out of her room, I'll get the others and we'll follow her."

"And me?"

"I will come for you," Lizard said. "I'm awfully sorry—we're all awfully sorry—about your daddy."

Greta's face seemed to crumple. She bent her head, then lifted it. When she spoke it was in her normal voice. "What if she doesn't spy walk tonight?"

"We're not sure," I said. "It may take a while before she goes up to the roof again, so we'll take turns staying awake and listening."

Maureen sighed. "I know it's for a good cause, but have you any idea what staying awake does to your looks? We'll have bags under our eyes, big ugly black ones. Ian won't like you anymore, Jessie. You'll look like an old crone. He won't want to kiss you, even if there's another air raid, even if it *is* in the dark."

"Shut up, Mo," Ada told her.

Maureen gazed into the distance. "I know. Phyllis Hollister has this special stuff. It's *for* bags. She sent away for the formula and made it herself in chemistry. You smooth it on like this." Maureen's sugary finger drew a white smudge under each eye. "Phyllis says it's sulfur and molasses and Egyptian oils."

"Where did she get those?" Ada asked, interested for the first time.

"Oh, she substituted cod liver oil. She stole it from the dispensary. Phyllis says cod liver oil is probably even better than Egyptian oils. She says that if it's so good for our insides, think what it'll do for our outsides."

Lizzie Mag shuddered. The smell of cod liver oil was awful.

"You'll stink us all out, Maureen," I said.

"If Miss Müller does go tonight," Greta said, as if she hadn't heard anything else, "and if we follow her and find her engaged in traitorous work, what is the plan then?"

"Well, we haven't really thought past finding her," I said.

"We'll say, 'Halt,' " Maureen said brightly. " 'Who goes there?' "

Greta gave her a disbelieving look. "The German will fight, you know. She will not be taken. Have you a plan for that?"

We looked at one another. Of course we had no plan for that. We had thought Miss Müller would meekly come with us.

"She might jump, of course," Greta said in a conversational way.

"You mean . . . off the roof?" Maureen's Arcs de Triomphe hoisted to high mast.

"No, she means through a hoop," Ada said. "Honestly, Maureen."

I swallowed nervously. "We could hold her and not let her go. There are four of us . . . I mean five."

"Criminy, she might pull us off the roof with her," Maureen said.

"Perhaps she will have a gun," Greta said.

"Oh, no." I tried for a laugh. "The maids would have found it. Maids find everything in this place."

"Not necessarily," Greta said. "Germans have ways of hiding things. They can hide hundreds of dead bodies. Hide them from the world. A little gun? Poof." She snapped her fingers.

"Dead bodies?" Maureen grabbed my pillow and held it over her face. "Did she say dead bodies?"

"We should consider," Greta went on. "It is best to be prepared and never to underestimate the enemy. That was the trouble with my people. We thought the Germans were human."

We were all quiet, sitting there on the bed. What awful

things Greta had seen and suffered. We couldn't begin to imagine them. It was a relief when the dressing bell clanged through the dorm. We had only fifteen minutes to change for high tea.

"You know which is my cubie?" Greta asked. "It is the first one by the door in Sleeping Beauty."

"I know," Lizzie Mag said. "We will not leave you behind, Greta. I promise."

I wished Lizard hadn't made that promise, because I was afraid of Greta. Hate is frightening.

"She's a load of fun," Maureen whispered sarcastically when Greta had left.

We were gathering up our debris, bundling the package together so Ada could give it to her brother Jack after tea.

"This is not supposed to be fun, Mo," I said. "It's dead earnest. Sometimes you're ridiculous."

Maureen looked offended. "Same to you with brass knobs on it," she said.

When they'd gone, I brushed the sugar off my quilt and began looking for my nail file to wipe it clean. It was nowhere. But it had to be. We'd just used it.

"Ada," I called. "Is my nail file still in the package for Jack? Would you look?"

I heard paper rustling. Ada called, "Not here. Check under your bed."

I checked there and all around. Under my quilt, under the things on my chair. The nail file, long and sharp as a dagger, had disappeared. Had someone taken it? Who? Could it have been Greta? But why? I didn't want to think what I was thinking.

12

"A LADY ALWAYS dresses for high tea," Old Rose said, so we had to throw off our gym tunics and blouses and black stockings and put on frocks. We were allowed to have two frocks, one to alternate with the other. "Excess is not in good taste," Old Rose told us. As Ada said, she should have taken a look at herself.

One of my frocks was dark red with a white collar, the other Alice blue cut in a princess line. I'd picked the styles from the Butterick Pattern Book, and Mrs. Reader, our Ballylo dressmaker, had "run them up" for me. Mrs. Reader knew everything about everybody, and she released it all to my mother through a mouthful of straight pins while she knelt adjusting my hems.

"Did you hear about Maggie Mulcahy? Another wee'un on the way and her with eight already." The pins shifted disapprovingly between Mrs. Reader's big yellow teeth. White threads clung like skinny worms to her black jumper. The tape measure around her neck quivered with indignation. "Old C.F. was full as the Boyne again last night, singing rebel songs. A terrible thing, the drink," she said, and her eyes flashed to my mother and away. She never mentioned my father and how he was drunk again last night, too, though she knew the way everyone in Ballylo knew.

Today I pulled the Alice blue frock from my wardrobe and put it on. My cousin Bryan said I looked thinner and older in it, so of course of the two it was my favorite. Bry had terrific taste. But I was thinking again about the nail file. Had Greta taken it? Or could it have slipped between the bed and the wall? I jerked the bed out and peered again beneath it. No use looking. She'd taken it, all right. Following Miss Müller had become ten times more dangerous since Greta got involved.

I peeled off my black stockings and put on my misty-morning lisle ones. Ada said the color was more like cow pats than morning mist, but Ada tended to see the worst in everything. I took my brown suede wedgies from my wardrobe shelf. They were my pride and joy. Wedgies were all the rage that year. We had bought mine in the Dolcis shoe store downtown. "The American look," twenty-four clothing coupons. To finish things off, I clipped on my single, understated string of cultured pearls.

The four of us—Lizzie Mag, Ada, Maureen, and I—walked to the dining room together. We weren't hungry, of course, after all that tuck, which was too bad because tonight was the best tea of the week—fried potato bread. The maids served us from platters, standing behind us, flinging the fried bread onto our plates. Usually we begged for seconds, like Oliver Twist. Usually the maids wouldn't give seconds. "A little power," Ada said, "is a dangerous and rotten thing."

Miss Müller wasn't at tea. The teachers had a Primus stove in their lounge and were allowed to make their own evening meal there if they preferred to. If I'd been Miss Müller, I'd have preferred to.

Down at the babies' end of the table the little first formers were hooting and howling, their hands over their mouths to smother their noise, their wicked little eyes darting around the table. Whatever they were up to seemed to involve Hillary and the pimply maid, Sarah Neely. She was hunched down beside Hillary having a giggly conversation. They'd both be in trouble if they were seen.

"Jessie?" Lizzie Mag leaned across the table. "Ian's making terrible googoo eyes at you. It's easy to see he's got a bad case of the lovesickness."

"Honestly?" My heart blipped a little blip.

"Here." Lizzie Mag shined her spoon on her napkin and reached it across to me. I held it up and tried to use it as a mirror since we weren't allowed to turn around to look. Sometimes if the light was right, and if I jiggled the spoon perfectly, I could get a glimpse of Ian, distorted but better than nothing. Tonight I couldn't see a thing.

The maids came along the table gathering up the silverware, so I had to surrender the spoon. At Alveara they were so scared we'd sneak something into our rooms that they cleared the tables before we'd eaten our last bites.

Already the prefects were setting up the cod liver oil tables across the two entrances. There was no escape in this world from cod liver oil. Mr. Bolton, who was the master on duty, said closing grace and ended it by saying, ". . . and for the oils of your big fish, so kindly provided, Lord, the boarders present are not terribly thankful." It made us all laugh. Honestly, Mr. Bolton was the nicest teacher in the world.

103

We lined up to get our spoonfuls. As soon as they took the tops off the big bottles, the whole dining room smelled like the bowels of a whaling ship. "Like we just harpooned Moby Dick," Ada said. We held our noses and opened our mouths. Lizzie Mag and I had vowed that if we were ever prefects at Alveara, we'd let some girls slip by, especially the ones who were almost boking on the way up the line. We had to say thank you to the prefects so they'd be certain we'd swallowed, though holding it in your mouth to spit out seemed a hundred times worse to me.

"And you're honestly going to put this stuff under your eyes, Mo?" Lizard asked. "What if the smell never comes off?"

"I'll suffer anything for beauty," Maureen said.

Ada had permission to stay behind and meet her brother to give him his share of the tuck. The rest of us milled back along the corridor to get our dressing gowns and put them over our frocks before we went to study hall. The hall was just one of the day classrooms with the heat turned off, and it was so cold that your breath froze in a cloud, and the rest of you froze right along with it.

"Carol Murchison's on study-hall duty," Lizzie Mag said, and rolled her eyes. "She'll keep us till the last minute and won't allow as much as a whisper."

"The only time I liked her was when she got the egg with the chicken in it this morning," Maureen said. "When she screamed, I realized she was a human being."

We got our dressing gowns and our books from our lockers, took our gas masks, and trailed back along the corridor. Boots was mopping the floor, and we hopped around the wet spots. "Don't slip, young ladies," he warned, and we called back, "We won't," even though we knew he couldn't hear us.

Lizzie Mag and I sat next to each other in a double desk, with Ada and Maureen directly behind. But Ada hadn't arrived yet. Two rows over I saw Greta Ludowski. She had her head bent over her French book, and though I stared and stared, she didn't look up. "Greta!" I hissed, and Carol Murchison, always on the alert at her desk in front, said: "Perhaps you aren't aware that study hall has started, Jessie Drumm. No talking, please."

We coughed, which was permitted, loudly slammed our books on the desks, whacked the pages open.

Carol's little beady eyes followed our every move.

In about five minutes Ada came, excused herself to Carol, and sat down. Immediately she touched my back. Something poked between my shoulders. Cautiously I put a hand back, brought it forward just as cautiously. It was an envelope. The name Jessie Drumm was written in little cramped writing on the front. A letter. Human instinct is an incredible thing. I knew instantly that it was from Ian. My stomach knew too, and gave a loud warning gurgle. Secretly, quietly, I opened the envelope.

"Dear Jessie," he wrote. "It was nice seeing you last night. I liked kissing you. I hope you had no ill effects. Ha ha. I hope we can see each other again. Yours sincerely, Ian McManus." I read it twice, then turned it over. He hoped I'd had no ill effects. Just a semi–heart attack and smoldering intestines, that was all.

I passed the letter under the desk to Lizzie Mag, who read, smiled, reached down, and squeezed my hand.

I slid it behind then and listened to the throb of silence as Ada and Mo read.

Ada whispered with her mouth right against my hair, "It's not exactly 'My love is like a red, red rose that's newly sprung in June.'" I could hardly hear her, but Carol, who had ears on her like a Belleek china jug, did. Her head came up fast.

"Ada Sinclair, were you whispering?"

"Yes, Carol."

"A hundred lines for tomorrow. 'I will not talk in study hall.'"

Ian's letter slid forward to me.

"Ada Sinclair, did you just pass something to Jessie Drumm?" Carol's voice quivered with anger. Carol prided herself on running a tight study hall. "Bring it up here this minute," she ordered.

"Oh, no," Lizard moaned.

Behind me I heard Ada whisper, "Eat it, Jessie. Quick. That's what spies do." I imagined the pulp clogging up my intestines if I ate it. I just couldn't. I sat with the letter under my hand.

"If Mohammed won't come to the mountain, the mountain will come to Mohammed," Carol announced, and came stalking toward me.

I scrunched up the letter and let it fall on the floor. Lizard kicked it quickly under the desk.

"Pick that up." Carol's voice was white with rage.

Lizard bent under cover of the desk. She gave me a despairing glance.

Carol held out her hand. "Give it to me."

I gave it.

As she walked back to her desk, I saw Carol uncrumpling my letter from Ian. My first-ever love letter that was so wonderful and so mine, not hers.

"Mean old biddy," Maureen hissed.

Carol whirled. "Who said that?"

"I did," Maureen said.

"One hundred lines. 'I will not talk in study hall.' "

"We'll help, Maureen," Ada whispered.

"Who said that?" Carol was beside herself.

"I did," Ada said.

"Another hundred lines from you, 'I will not talk in study hall.' "

"We'll help, Ada," Lizard said.

Carol was about to have apoplexy. Before she could ask her famous question, there was a chorus of "We'll help" all around study hall.

Carol's apoplexy was about to choke her. "One hundred lines from everybody, due tomorrow. If I had the authority to give you detention, I would give it."

"You bet she would," someone said.

"Who said that?" Carol asked.

"We did," a dozen voices answered.

"Make that two hundred lines for tomorrow—from everybody."

Carol had reached her desk. She frowned down at Ian's crumpled letter, then she frowned at me. "This is very serious," she said. "I think we would all benefit from hearing this epistle and recognizing its implications."

"Please, Carol." Lizzie Mag was standing, her face flushed pink. Lizard is not one for speaking up, so I was astonished. "It is not fair to read other people's mail," she said.

"This letter couldn't have been too private," Carol said. "I see it is addressed 'Jessie Drumm,' but you were all reading it." Carol was skinny and her red-checked frock made her look like a brick chimney and just as immovable.

"We had Jessie's permission," Lizard said in her little voice, so little now that Carol had to crane her head to hear. "Excuse me, Carol, but you don't have Jessie's permission."

"I don't need permission for anything that goes on in my study hall," Carol said in the most superior voice I'd ever heard. "Sit down, Lizzie Mag."

Lizzie sat. I gave her a smile of thanks, but it was pretty weak. I was dying.

Lizard nudged me and whispered, "Look, Jessie."

I looked. Every single girl in study hall had her fingers in her ears, even Mean Jean Ross. Everyone except Greta Ludowski. She was staring around study hall, very alert and with a strange questioning look on her face. Now everyone was humming. The room sounded like a busy beehive.

Carol's mouth moved. I think she said, "Take your fingers out of your ears this minute and be quiet," but it was hard to tell. She glared at us. Then she read the letter, but all the words were drowned in the buzzing.

At the end she sat down. She put the envelope on the edge of the desk and motioned for me to come get it.

I did.

As I walked back, all fingers came out of all ears and the humming stopped.

"Get on with your homework," Carol Murchison said in a voice so cold it frosted the air around her face. "And don't think you've heard the last of this," she added.

"Tee hee," Ada whispered.

If that was a quotation, I didn't recognize it. I knew

Carol had heard it, but she didn't want to start anything new. For the moment she was defeated.

I wriggled my fingers behind me in all directions to thank my friends, but I did it secretly so the wrath of Carol wouldn't fall on us again. Then I opened my geometry book.

It was bad sometimes being a boarder, but sometimes it was nice. Ada said we'd stay best friends all our lives because we were like sisters, only better. Lizzie Mag said when we were grown up her parents would be home from India and we'd all live on the same street and she'd be auntie to my children and I'd be auntie to hers. And we'd love them to bits. "A big, big family," she said, "all of us."

I smiled over my isosceles triangle. Auntie Jessie. Uncle Ian.

Carol was biting her nails and looking as if she'd swallowed a crab. She'd tell all the other prefects about my letter from Ian. The thought made me cringe, but not for long. As Maureen would say, "Jealous, jealous, jealous." I bet none of the prefects had ever had a love letter from someone as smashing as Ian McManus.

I finished my geometry and started on my two hundred lines. Thirty-two done. "I will not talk in study hall. I will not talk . . ." When ending bell rang, Carol stood up.

"I'm supposed to remind all of you that last night we had an air raid. There could be another one tonight."

"Oh boy . . . boys!" Maureen whispered behind me. But I was remembering the direct hit and the house that had disappeared and the man who had had to go to Purdysburn. The idea of another raid, even it if meant being kissed again, wasn't so great. There had to be an easier way.

"You are to be sure to have your emergency cases properly packed," Carol went on. "Miss Rose says there may be an inspection *anytime*, and contraband found in any case will be confiscated and the girl punished."

She looked with satisfaction around the room. "I am to remind you also that if we do go to the shelters, there is to be no unseemly behavior. Any girl caught doing what Pearl Carson did—"

Ada interrupted. "Could you please tell us what she did, Carol? We aren't sure, and if we're to avoid—"

"Be quiet, Ada Sinclair." Carol glared at us silently, then said, "All of you, two hundred lines tomorrow night. You may leave."

"Thank you, Carol." We sounded meek as mice but we were triumphant mice.

We clattered our belongings together and headed down the corridor.

"It was Maureen who started the ear plugging and humming," Lizard said, patting Maureen on the back.

I gave Maureen a quick hug. "Thanks, Mo."

"Imagine our girl having that much gumption," Ada said. "Have you been taking gumption lessons, Mo?"

"I have natural ability. I just keep it hidden," Maureen said.

I was looking around for Greta, and when I saw her walking along as usual, I whispered to the others to go on. "I have to talk to her," I said.

Greta glanced at me when I caught up to her but she didn't speak.

"I'd like to have my nail file back," I said.

She didn't answer. Once, when she first came, I would

have thought she didn't understand, but now I knew she understood perfectly.

"It was interesting what happened in study hall tonight," Greta said in a dreamy kind of voice. "Dictators win in the beginning, but if everyone stands together, if everyone fights together, then a dictator can be defeated. That is what we hope."

She was walking fast and I had trouble keeping up. The cords of my dressing gown had come untied and I was tripping on them. There was no way I could retie them unless I stopped and put down my books.

"Listen," I said. "I know you took my nail file and I know why. If you don't give it back, we won't come for you when we follow Miss Müller. We're not planning on hurting her, we just want to find out what she's doing."

Greta smiled. "We *will* find out," she said. "And I will be there, whether you come for me or not. I promise you that."

13

PARTWAY ALONG THE corridor there was a little room that we called halfway house. We could stop there on our way back to the dorm from study hall and get a glass of milk from the big white jugs the maids left out. The first and second and third formers were dismissed from their study halls before we were. So halfway house was always a mess of used glasses and half-empty jugs. There were always pools of spilled milk on the table and on the floor, too.

I stopped at the room, but Greta went on. I didn't think we had anything more to say to each other.

Lizzie Mag and Maureen and Ada were waiting for me outside the door, and I told them what Greta had said.

Lizzie Mag frowned. "But what did she mean, she'd be there whether we came for her or not? How would she know which night?"

"Maybe she means she'll be there in spirit, like God," Maureen suggested.

We stared.

"Well, you know when he said, 'Lo I am with you always,' and I asked Reverend Patton in Bible school how that could be, and Reverend Patton said it was God's spirit that was with us always."

We were aghast. Ada made the Catholic cross sign on herself and said, "You'll be struck dead, Maureen Campbell, comparing Greta Ludowski to God."

"I never . . ." Maureen began.

"Mo didn't mean it like that," Lizzie Mag said quickly. "She just meant Greta would be with us in her thoughts, because of her father."

"Of course that's what I meant," Maureen said. "You are so dense, Ada. Do you think I'd be rude to God? I think God is great." She looked at us, baffled.

"We know, Maureen." I turned to Lizzie Mag. "You did promise you'd go and get Greta when we follow Miss Müller, but you won't, will you?"

Lizard shook her head. "Not if Greta's going to hurt her."

"Well, we're on our own again," I told the others. But I was remembering Greta's voice, the way she smiled, and I wasn't so sure.

"I want milk," Ada said, "if those greedy little kids have left any."

"Phyllis Hollister said if I came right away, she'd give me some of her eye-bag stuff," Maureen told us. "I'm going. See you in the dorm."

The three of us went in. Halfway house was crowded and right away everyone began asking me about Ian's letter.

"Come on, Jessie, share. We know it was from him. Did he say he loved you?" They moaned and closed their eyes and staggered about, holding their hearts and knocking over the almost-empty milk pitchers.

It turned out Mean Jean Ross hadn't plugged her ears all the way. She fingered her big silver cross and announced, "He told her he liked kissing her, I can tell you that much."

"He also said Mean Jean Ross has a mouth like a barbed-wire fence and no boy boarder would be caught dead kissing *her*," Ada said quickly. "Pass it on."

"He did not, and same to your mouth and double it over," Mean Jean shouted.

"Let's go," I whispered to Lizard. The three of us picked up our books and gas masks and started back to the dorm. My fingers smoothed Ian's letter in my dressing-gown pocket and I thought it was sort of nice to be teased about it. As far as I knew, and I *would* know, I was the first in my form to get a letter from a boy. It made me feel special.

"Maybe tonight will be the night Miss Müller goes," Lizzie Mag said as we walked along the second half of the corridor.

I nodded.

"Well, thank heaven we're not going to have to watch the Fräulein and Greta, too," Ada said. "That would have been a muck-up." She wrinkled her nose and stopped. "What is that smell?"

Afterward we decided we'd smelled the smell the second we entered Long Parlor, but we were so busy thinking of Greta and Miss Müller that nobody had said anything about it.

"It must be Maureen's stuff." Lizzie was trying to wriggle her nose into the collar of her dressing gown.

"That is just about the worst smell I ever smelled," Ada said. "Except once when a rat died in our storeroom

114

behind a bag of meal and we didn't find it for three weeks."

"Don't make it worse," I begged.

We dropped our books and gas masks on the dorm floor and Ada bellowed for Maureen. She came out of her cubie looking guilty. Under each eye was a thick plaster of sticky, shiny black.

"Heaven preserve us!" Ada clamped her fingers around her nose.

"It's just sulfur and molasses and oils . . . and Phyllis said she added a little bit of butter because the mixture wouldn't spread and—"

"The butter's spoiled, Mo," Lizard croaked. Her face had turned a pretty shade of leaf green.

Ada pushed past Maureen. "Where is the stuff?"

Maureen rushed after her. "It's in my soap dish, but don't you dare touch it. I paid Phyllis two shillings for it."

"You what?" I said. "That was supposed to be your contribution for this week's war bonds."

Ada came out of Mo's cubie holding the soap dish at arm's length.

"I promise I'll get a jar for it tomorrow," Maureen said. "Phyllis had hers in a jar. It's probably smelly because the air has some chemical effect."

"It's *steaming*," Lizard whispered.

"It's *bubbling*," I said, trying not to breathe.

Ada dashed to the bathroom with Maureen on her heels. We heard the lavatory flush and then the tap running full tilt.

Lizard groaned. "But the smell's still here. It's awful."

"No windows to open," I moaned.

"Well, it's not on Maureen anymore," Ada said, pushing Mo in front of her. Maureen's face had been washed clean. "I told her we'll pay back her two shillings among us, not that she deserves it."

Lizzie Mag had picked up her lesson book and fanned it hard in front of her face.

"I know," I said. "Let's put on our gas masks."

We pulled them out of their cases and wiggled them on, breathing in their rubbery stuffiness, pointing at each other and laughing smothered laughs. We looked like a bunch of black, long-snouted pigs.

Ada made pig noises that sounded so good, we all began grunting and crawling around on the floor.

"Dicks! Dicks!" Someone called from the bathroom, warning that a teacher or prefect was coming, and we struggled to our feet.

"Uh-oh," we muttered, remembering what Old Rose had said. "Gas masks are not toys. They are never to be used inappropriately or for anything other than their intended function, which is to insure your survival should the Germans drop poison gas." Old Rose had said it more than once.

We pulled and tugged at them. Gas masks clamped themselves to your skin, which is what they were supposed to do, and you had to peel them off. They came away like limpets from a rock.

We were still struggling with them when Bengie came into the dorm. This meant trouble.

Bengie watched us. "What is that awful smell?" she said.

"We thought maybe the Germans had dropped poison gas," Ada said quickly. "We thought we should protect ourselves as best we—"

"Ada, give over," Bengie said in a sort of absent-minded way. She was looking at me.

"Jessie?"

It was amazing the meaning that one ordinary word could have. It was more amazing how my stomach got the message so quickly since it had to go all the way from my ears to my brain first.

"What?" I asked, stopping with the gas mask half stuffed into its case.

"Miss Rose wants to see you in her sitting room," Bengie said.

"Now?" I felt Lizzie Mag move closer to me, felt her shoulder touch mine.

"Did that Carol go and blab and tattle about Jessie's letter?" Maureen asked. "It didn't take her long to get to Old Rose."

"Carol Murchison, Gestapo agent," Ada said.

Lizzie Mag took my gas mask from my hands and said, "I'll do this for you, Jess."

And then Bengie said, "You're to come right away, Jessie."

There was such a hollow feeling inside me.

"Good luck," Ada said as Bengie and I left, and Lizard said, "I'll put your books in your cubie, Jess."

I walked fast to keep up as Bengie strode along the corridor.

"Is it about—" I began.

Bengie didn't slow. "All I know, Jess, is you had a telephone call from home."

"What?" I stopped. "It's not about the letter? But . . . from home?"

The cord on my dressing gown had come untied again

117

and I tripped over it. "But Bengie, it's so late. It's after eight. They never call this late. Something must be wrong."

"I don't know. . . ." Bengie took the dressing-gown cord from me and tied the ends neatly in front, just where my stomach was starting to cramp really badly. I didn't like the gentle way she did it, as if she knew something bad and was sorry for me. Now she was hurrying again. I could tell she didn't want to talk, didn't want to have to answer questions.

Last night we'd all come along this corridor on our way to the shelter, the sound of bombs falling around us, but I was more frightened now. "Is it Daddy?" I whispered. Maybe Bengie didn't hear me, because she didn't answer. I had this instant picture of him, drunk on a road, a car running over him, or his liver splitting from the drink. Dr. Conway had warned him about his liver. "It's pickled like a herring, Magnus," Dr. Conway had said. "One of these days it's just going to explode."

We'd reached the door of Old Rose's sitting room. From the walls of the front hall the portraits of the former headmistresses gazed down at me, uncaring. They were dead. They weren't worrying about anybody now.

"Are you okay?" Bengie asked gently.

I nodded and knocked on the door.

Old Rose was sitting by the fire, her radio playing some soft music, it might have been "Clair de Lune." I think it was the Palm Court Orchestra, or maybe the BBC Light Programme. A tray was on a small table beside her. It held a jug of cocoa and a blue plate of digestive biscuits arranged in a circle. There were two blue mugs.

"Hello, precious." She held out a hand without getting up, and I had to go across and take it. She did that sometimes. Ada said Old Rose thought she was the Archbishop of York and we should kneel to be blessed.

"What a pleasure it is, Jessie, seeing you twice in one day." Her voice was so sweet it scared me more. Why was she being so sweet? Normally she wasn't sweet at all. "Your dear mother phoned, and though it is late I gave permission for you to phone her back."

My throat was dry. "Is it . . . has something happened to my father?"

"No, *no*, precious. As far as I am aware, your mother and father are perfectly fine. Why don't you just speak to them. . . ." She let go of my hand and waved toward the phone. She didn't ask me to sign the book. She didn't remind me to keep the conversation short. She even turned her chair so she was looking at the fire and not at me. Something was very wrong.

My fingers trembled as I dialed. There was no view of the grounds tonight. The blackout curtains were closed, hanging in thick folds. The lamp dripped a small pool of light over Old Rose's chair. I could see the top of her head, the finger wave she always had put in her hair that looked like the ripples at the edge of Lough Neagh.

"Jessie?" My father's voice, sober, steady, gentle.

"Yes, Daddy?"

"I have bad news." With one hand I held the edge of the table.

"The War Office sent your aunt Clara and uncle Eammon a telegram," my father said. And then he told me that my cousin Bryan had been taken prisoner by the Germans. That he was a prisoner of war.

14

I COULD IMAGINE my cousin Bryan in some cell, Nazi soldiers kicking him with those high polished boots they wear. No sun, no air. Bread and water. A hole under the ground.

I couldn't bear it. I gnawed at my knuckles.

My father said he and my mother were driving early in the morning to Enniskillen to be with Aunt Clara and Uncle Eammon. They'd got an extra compassionate ration of petrol from the Ministry of Transportation. My father said there'd be a list of Northern Ireland soldiers taken prisoner in the *Belfast Newsletter* in the morning.

"We were afraid someone might tell you about it, or ask you, darlin', Bryan's last name being Drumm same as yours. And it not a usual name at all. Not like Johnson," he joked, and I knew he was trying to cheer me up because he always told me how lucky I was to have a distinguished name like Drumm and not my mother's family name, Johnson. I swallowed. Bryan Drumm, prisoner of war. Maybe he'd only be a number now.

"Are you still there, darlin'?"

"Yes."

I wanted to be home. To have my arms around my daddy's neck. To cry.

"Oh, darlin', your mother and I know how much you love Bry."

I nodded, though he couldn't see me. Bryan was the brother I didn't have, the friend who understood about Daddy. The one I could talk to and who could comfort and advise me.

"Miss Rose thought it best that we talk to you ourselves tonight, Jess. She was very good, so she was."

"Daddy, will you tell everyone how sorry I am." I choked back my tears. "Tell them I'll be writing to them."

"I will. Would you like to speak to Mummy?"

"No. It's all right." I didn't think I could talk anymore. My throat hurt and my ears, too. Why did my ears ache?

"I will not take a drop of the stuff, Jessie," my father said in a low, tight voice. "I'm promising you that. They'll all need me. I mean it, Jess."

"Good." I knew he meant it. I was almost sure he wouldn't be able to do it. The thought made my throat and ears ache even more. "Good night, Daddy."

Old Rose turned her chair. It was on those little wheel things so it turned easily. "Come here, precious," she said, and stood up and enfolded me in her arms. She was soft as a cushion. My nose was filled with the smell of stale face powder and stale perfume. Her hair, washboard stiff, scratched against my cheek. Ada always said the waves were sculpted in cement.

"There, there, there," she whispered. Part of me was wailing for Bryan. The other part was staggered by all this. Old Rose and I hugging.

She let me go and held me away from her. Her little green eyes were soft and swimming in their own tears. "Sit down here, love." She patted the thick flower-patterned seat of one of the big chairs. "You and I are going to have a nice cup of cocoa."

I watched the cocoa stream, brown and frothy, into the two blue mugs while I sank into the chair. My dressing gown hung open. My misty-morning lisle stockings were dusty on the knees where I'd been crawling around on the dorm floor being a pig. The toes of my brown suede wedgies were scuffed. I rubbed them one at a time against the trail of my dressing gown. All those clothing coupons they'd required. Bryan had never even seen my wedgies. He would have liked them.

"Biscuit, darling?" Old Rose passed me the plate. I took one. The turf fire sparked and glowed red and peaceful in its depths. The music wrapped itself around us.

"Your father told me Bryan is your favorite cousin," Old Rose said.

I broke off a piece of biscuit. "Yes." Oh, thank goodness my father had been sober when he'd called and not talking nonsense. Usually my mother kept him and Old Rose separated. She kept him separated from just about anyone outside of Ballylo. Inside Ballylo was like his own big drunken playpen.

"Bryan's young and strong, Jessie," Old Rose said. "He'll have the will to survive." She sighed. "His wonderful years of youth are being stolen from him, and that's a tragedy. But war is a tragedy."

The lights-out bell sounded and I set down my half-drunk mug of cocoa on the hearth beside Gog, or maybe it was Magog, and half stood.

Old Rose waved her hand. "You are allowed to stay up late tonight. I arranged for Miss Müller to put the torch lamp in your room so you can see to get undressed."

The torch lamp was the little battery-run lamp that was placed on the cubie dresser if a girl had the runs and had to go to the lavatory a few times in the night, or maybe if a girl was having a nightmare. It was a rare occurrence, though. I wondered if Old Rose had told Miss Müller about Bry. Your rotten, murdering Huns got him, I thought. They've taken my cousin. Hitler has stolen the years of his youth.

"Sit down and be comfortable, Jessie," Old Rose said. She offered another biscuit and I took it, crumbling it between my fingers, catching the crumbs before they could drop into the chair.

Old Rose lay back and closed her eyes and we were quiet. The music was nice.

"It's called *La Mer* and it's by Debussy," she told me, moving a hand dreamily. "It makes me think of days by the sea when I was a child. We always spent our holidays in Cushendun." Old Rose had been a child? How strange this all was, as if she really cared about me. Maybe she did. Maybe she cared about all of us in her actressy way.

She opened her eyes. "How do you feel, Jessie? Does your stomach hurt? Shall I ring for Nursie to give you something?"

"No, please." The thought of milk of magnesia was more than I could bear.

"Well, we'll just sit quietly for a little while then and let the music soothe us." She stirred up the fire with the big poker. White ashes drifted like snow and settled below the grate.

I sat there and tried to imagine the sea, but instead I thought about Bryan, about the last time he'd taken me up to Glenshane Pass on the back of his big Norton 350

123

motorcycle. The way his cheeks were so red and his hair, curly as mine, stood up like a paintbrush.

When the piece ended and a man's voice came on to tell us what was next, Old Rose stood and said gently: "Perhaps you should run along now, darling. Have a good cry. Crying helps mend the heart, but never quite." She kissed my forehead. "If you want to talk anytime, I am here. I am your friend. And tomorrow you may come right after last period and you may phone your parents. I have the number in Enniskillen where they will be."

"Thank you, Miss Rose."

She was my friend. Right now I believed that absolutely. But still I backed my way out of her room.

Alveara lay quiet. It must have been half an hour ago that the lights-out bell had sounded. All the girls would be in bed, the little ones long ago. There'd be nobody around except teachers and maybe a prefect or two. They could stay up till ten, ten thirty on weekends. Lizzie Mag and I were looking forward to that part of being prefects, if we ever made it.

I went fast along the corridor, the clip-clop of my wedgies echoing against the walls. It was spooky at night with the door of halfway house open and all the tables and shelves swabbed down and empty, and the stairs to the basement shelter disappearing into the darkness below.

I hurried through Long Parlor. The bad smell was still there. I'd forgotten about it, but now it seemed even worse. I found a hanky in my pocket and held it against my nose. It was gritty with digestive-biscuit crumbs, and it was damp, too, where I'd wiped my eyes.

Long Parlor was dark except for the faint light that filtered in from the bathroom at the top of the dorms. Magazines had spilled from the table onto the floor. I saw the one with the picture of Betty Grable on the cover. Maybe it was *Life*. We hardly read anything in *Life*, or *Time* either, except the film-star features.

Tomorrow I'd ask Mr. Bolton to let me see his *Belfast Newsletter*. He always walked down and got it at the end of the drive in the little shop next to the College Chemists. I'd find Bryan's name in the paper. Maybe Mr. Bolton would let me cut it out. I could fold it and keep it in my blazer pocket. Oh, Bryan . . .

On the long vinyl sofa at the far end of Long Parlor a shadow moved. My heart stopped, started again with a jerk. Somebody there. Something. The ghost of Marjorie? I wanted to run, but as in the dream I had sometimes, I couldn't move.

"Is anybody there?" I was poised for flight on one foot like the statue of the Greek god with wings on his ankles. "Who . . . who is it?"

"It's Greta Ludowski." A flashlight came on, the beam fixing itself to me. "I knew it was you, Jessie," Greta said.

"What are you doing?" I couldn't make sense out of why she was in Long Parlor after lights-out. My head seemed full of fuzz.

She turned out the flashlight and the dark was blacker than ever. "I'm going to sleep here . . . or not sleep," Greta said.

"You can't."

"I can. Nobody will know. Nobody will see me here on this black sofa. You would not have seen me if I hadn't allowed it. I will be back in my bed in the morning."

I fumbled for reasons. "You'll be in trouble if you're caught. And you'll freeze."

"I don't worry about trouble and I brought the blanket from my bed. Besides, I have slept in worse places."

"You're . . ." I stopped, knowing suddenly why she was here.

"Yes, I'm waiting for Miss Müller to go to bed and then to come back out. She will not leave Snow White tonight without me seeing her."

I heard the squeak of the sofa as she lay down again. Was my nail file tight in her hand, at the ready?

"You had a phone call? It was bad news?" Greta asked.

"Yes. My cousin has been taken prisoner by the Germans."

"I am sorry, but be grateful he is not dead," she said.

I folded my hanky thicker. "That smell is really awful. Maureen was an idiot to use the stuff."

"Yes. It bothers me, too. I would be fine in here if I didn't have to breathe."

Was she making a joke? No, Greta Ludowski didn't make jokes.

There was more squeaking on the sofa and I knew somehow that she had turned her back to me, that she'd said all she was going to say.

"Well, good night," I said. "I'll be listening for Miss Müller too."

"It doesn't matter if you do or not," Greta said. "I will take care of her."

15

IT WAS DARK in the dorm, too, the light from the bath-room making a blueness in the space between the cubies. A faint glow hung above my room . . . the torch lamp. The smell was everywhere. It wasn't keeping Maureen awake, though. Her snores thumped and dwindled, thumped and dwindled. I tried to tiptoe in case Ada and Lizzie Mag were asleep too, but it wasn't easy to tiptoe in wedgies.

Girl boarders were not allowed to walk barefoot or in socks or stockings. "Shoes or slippers at all times," Old Rose said. It was in case of verrucas. Old Rose said ver-rucas thrived on the soles of feet. They were hard as lentils, and walking on them was like walking on gravel for the rest of your life, because there was no known cure, and worst of all, verrucas had hair growing out of them.

My father said there was no such thing and no such word. Old Rose was just scaring us out of going bare-foot. It worked. Mention verrucas and Maureen had a conniption fit. They were the terror of her life. "Imagine," she said, propping a foot up on her dresser and examining it carefully in the mirror, "imagine Charles Boyer or Alan

Ladd taking off your satin slipper so he can drink champagne from it. He tenderly lifts your little foot in his hand and begins to kiss it, and here's this great big hairy thing sprouting out of the bottom. Wouldn't you die?"

"As dead as a kipper," Ada agreed.

Now I tiptoed as quietly as I could in wedgies.

Ten seconds after I got to my cubie, Lizzie Mag came in. Her hair was in its neat row of pin curls and her face shone with Pond's cold cream.

Ada arrived two seconds later. She had a little farther to come.

"What did Old Rose say about the letter?" Lizzie Mag asked. "Are you in terrible trouble, Jess?"

"We're sending that sneak Carol Murchison to Coventry for telling," Ada said. "Nobody in the whole of the fourth form is going to as much as speak to her for a fortnight."

I bit my lips. "It wasn't about the letter," I said, and I told them about Bryan. I'd begun sniffling again, though I didn't want to because sniffling brought the awful smell all the way to the top of my nose and just about made me choke.

"We should kill Maureen for making this smell," I muttered. I reached for my towel and wiped my eyes. When I took my hanky out for a blow, it was too damp and crumby to use. Ada pulled some sheets of Alveara toilet paper from her pajama pocket. It was the worst toilet paper in the world, dark brown and hard, so rough Ada said she once used it to sand down a splintery place on her dresser. She hoarded it for getting the mud off her shoes, and Maureen used it to smooth the skin on her legs. We called it "the last resort" because most of

128

the time we brought our own toilet paper rolls from home.

"I'm okay," I sniffled, and used the sleeve of my good Alice blue frock to dab gently at what remained of my nose after blowing it on the last resort.

"I'm awful sorry about Bryan," Lizzie Mag said. "Oh, poor Jessie."

Ada gritted her little square teeth. "I'm sorry too. Those rotten Huns. The bad is in them, as big as a bull."

I nodded.

Then I told them about Greta on watch in Long Parlor.

Lizzie Mag gave a little shiver. "Will she stay there every night till Miss Müller goes out again?"

"I suppose."

Ada jerked her thumb at Maureen's cubie. "That one whined and yelped and said she couldn't get over being responsible for the smell, and she swore she wouldn't sleep a wink, what with the smell and her bad conscience. She's either sleeping or she's playing piggie in her gas mask again."

"Jess," Lizzie Mag said, "I know you said you'd do first turn watching Miss Müller tonight, but I'll take your place. You don't need to be awake and thinking about Bry."

"That's okay." I smiled at Lizard. "I don't think I'll sleep anyway."

"I've got *Lady Chatterley's Lover*," Ada said. "Jack lent it to me after tea. We should all read it, he says. He says it'll change our innocence forever. Keep your fingers crossed that he's right." Ada turned to me. "You can borrow it first for tonight, Jess. I can lend you my flashlight—the batteries are great."

"It's okay. Thanks."

We froze at a sudden sound outside. "Dicks!" Ada whispered. "It's Miss Müller." We heard her footsteps getting closer.

"Oh, Jess, she's coming to your room," Lizard said. She and Ada ducked behind my door.

"Jessie?" Miss Müller opened the door a few inches. "You are not yet undressed? I understand you had sad news tonight."

"Yes."

Safe in her hiding place, Ada made devil's horns above her head.

"I am very sorry." Miss Müller's voice was absolutely empty. She wasn't sorry at all. Bryan was just another British soldier out of the way. One less to fight against her precious Germans.

Maybe I wouldn't have said what I said if Ada and Lizzie Mag hadn't been there listening. If Ada hadn't been waggling her devil horns. But maybe I would have said it anyway, thinking of how Miss Müller wasn't really a bit sorry about Bryan.

"Please don't tell me how *we* take *you* Germans prisoner too," I said. "But we treat our prisoners well. You beat them and whip them and starve them . . . and probably even *torture* them." I couldn't stand what I was imagining. Bry. Bry being tortured.

Miss Müller put her hand to her forehead. "Good night," she said. "I am going to bed too." The door closed.

Ada waved her fist triumphantly as she came out of her hiding place. "Smashing," she said. "You told her."

"We'd better go," Lizard said softly. "Unless you want

130

me to stay with you for a while, Jessie. I will if you want."

There was a new sound outside, a sort of dull plop. Then Miss Müller screamed and there was a rush of loud words in German, the most awful wailing kind of words I had ever heard.

Maureen's snores stopped, but they started again, like a drumbeat as the three of us rushed across the dorm to Miss Müller's room.

The smell was awful. Worse now, a hundred times worse.

The door was wide open. Miss Müller stood just inside. Something foul was spattered on her shoulder and down the front of her blue suit. The something was pale yellow and orange and black and oozing.

"Oh, boke!" Ada reeled back. "Oh, stinko, boko!"

Miss Müller's back was to us but I could see her in the dresser mirror, see the frozen, disbelieving look on her face. "It is too much," she whispered. "Too much."

I bit on my thumb. "What is it?"

"Holy Christmas," Ada said, semi-recovered. "It's the chicken and the egg."

"It's all over her."

Lizard took a step toward Miss Müller, but Ada caught her arm and pulled her back.

"Look at the chicken—it's on her shoulder," Ada said. "It looks exactly like a dried-up dead mouse."

It was. It did. My stomach heaved.

Miss Müller stood the way the mannequins stand in the window of Robinson Cleavers department store, her head stiff, her hands held out at her sides, palms up.

"Oh, Miss Müller. How awful." Lizard pushed past

Ada. "Give me some of the last resort, Ada." Lizard doesn't speak loudly, but somehow she has the kind of voice you obey.

"Lizzie Mag, you are a dope," Ada said, but she fished a wad of last resort from her pajama pocket and Lizard peeled off a piece and covered the dried-up chicken with it and pouched it into the paper. She took another piece and dabbed up the glob that was stuck in Miss Müller's hair. Ada and I watched.

Miss Müller spoke in a stream of spaced-out words, as if each one was separated from the next by a hyphen. "You-girls-get-back-to-bed. Your-trick-worked."

"We didn't do it," I said.

Ada squinted up. "It must have been balanced on the top of the door; the door probably wasn't closed all the way, and when you opened it . . ."

"Go-now," Miss Müller said, no part of her moving. I don't think even her lips moved. "Each-to-her-own-cubicle-please."

We went. Lizzie Mag still had the two pieces of toilet paper, one of them with the dead chicken inside. She ran to the bathroom and flushed it.

I got undressed and into my pajamas. I was shaking and cold and miserable. Ian's letter was still in my dressing-gown pocket, and I got out of bed again and slipped it under my pillow. Maybe it would help to make me feel better, but I didn't think even that could.

I reached for my bottle of Evening in Paris cologne and sprinkled a little around to disguise the smell, which was unbelievable, especially now that I knew what it was. Then I switched off the torch lamp and lay back. My head was jammed with thoughts . . . of Bryan, of Miss

Müller, of Old Rose, of Greta. Had she come to the dorm to watch during the commotion? If she had, she'd stayed well back. She'd be very pleased about the egg. Her dark eyes had probably sparkled with delight.

Oh, cripes. Miss Müller was leaving her room. My heart pounded and I got out of bed so fast I almost tripped. I eased open the door and peered out. She was going toward the bathroom in her dressing gown, walking in the slant of blue light, carrying her towel and soap dish. Of course she'd have to wash, wouldn't she?

Lizzie Mag's head popped up over the cubie wall, and when I stood on my dresser top I saw Ada was up on her dresser, too. "She's gone to the bathroom," Lizard said. "Do you think it was Greta put the egg on her door?"

"Good job if she did," Ada said, and Maureen's snore went hrrrumph in agreement.

"I think it was Hillary Walker," I told them. "She and the little maid Sarah Neely were talking at tea. I thought Hillary was up to something. I'm sure she got Sarah to get the egg for her."

"You mean little Hillary Walker thought of this? Hillary Walker, the first former?" Ada hit her forehead with her hand. "Gee, we should write and tell King George about her. She should get the Order of the British Empire, at least."

"It was a rotten thing to do," Lizzie Mag said quietly.

"You're too softhearted, Lizard," Ada told her.

"I didn't have a chance to tell you how nice Old Rose was to me tonight," I said to change the subject. "She even hugged me."

"In the grip of the lowland gorilla," Ada said.

"No, she was very . . ." I stopped. "Does it seem as if

133

Miss Müller's been in the bathroom a long time? She couldn't have slipped away to do more of her spy stuff, could she? Through Cinderella? Or Sleeping Beauty?" I slid down from my dresser and into the dorm.

Ada and Lizzie crowded behind me. "Should we waken Mo?" Ada asked.

"Let's check first," I said.

We went silent as snakes, but we didn't have to. The gurgle of the never-ending lavatory system seemed louder tonight, and it would have covered just about anything.

I was first, and I stopped the other two with a warning hand.

The bathroom was awash in its usual cold blue light that left the ceiling dark with cobwebs and shadows. The tubs had been filled earlier with their icy water in case of incendiary bombs. Miss Müller sat, facing away from us, in one of the tubs.

Usually there was a big wooden-handled scrub brush hanging on the side wall. We were supposed to use it and the bar of harsh Monkey Brand soap that sat with it to wash the dirty ring off the tub when we finished bathing. Miss Müller had the brush and the soap in the bath with her. She sat in icy water up to her waist, scrubbing herself. Even from here I could see the red streaks the brush bristles had left on her shoulders and back. The scene was like a painting by some weird modern artist, a painting filled with horror and despair.

We turned and ran.

16

ADA AND LIZZIE MAG and I stood in the dorm. Lizzie Mag was trembling. "Poor Miss Müller," she whispered.

Ada slitted her eyes. "Poor nothing. She's doing penance. Old-time monks and friars used to do that to repent of their sins, except they used whips and called it flagellation. I think it's Catholic."

"Still," I whispered, shivering too. I was remembering the way Miss Müller had said, "I can't help being half German." But she was. And it was her friends, her father's friends, who'd taken my Bryan prisoner. I hardened my heart. "We'd better be in our cubies when she comes back," I said.

Ada lifted one foot and hopped to examine it. "We've probably got hundreds of verrucas."

"I don't think Miss Müller will go spy walking tonight," Lizzie Mag said, and I shook my head. "I think she's had enough for anyone."

We whispered our good nights.

In about ten minutes I heard Miss Müller come back from the bathroom. Her door closed. Her lamp went off. Above our heads, up by the high ceiling where the darkness slept, the smell still hung, faint and putrid. I wondered what Miss Müller had done with the blue suit. She'd probably rolled it up to take to the cleaners.

Miss Müller was hiccuping softly, or maybe crying, little soft, stifled sobs. I put the edge of the sheet between my teeth and tried humming inside my head so I wouldn't hear. Wasn't it great the way the girls had all hummed for me in study hall tonight? I still had my two hundred lines to finish. I'd have to do them tomorrow in my free period.

Miss Müller was still crying. The night I'd cried about my daddy, she'd come into my cubie and stroked my hair and talked. Was anyone else awake listening to those little stifled sounds? I couldn't stand it. My crystal set was in my emergency case under my bed. I got up and found it, remembering that I hadn't repacked the case for another raid, or an inspection. They'd get me. Oh well, I didn't care.

I spread the crystal set out on my quilt, using my flashlight to sort out the wires. Ada's brother had sold the set to me for a pound. The boys made them in woodworking class. Mine was a real dud, but it was better than nothing. I put the earplug in my ear and moved the diode to bring in the stations. Snatches of this and that came through, and then I heard Lord Haw Haw's voice, plummy, the way it always was, fake British. He was actually Irish with an English accent, and he broadcast for the Germans, the traitor.

"Good people of London, it is sad to think of what you must endure night after night," Lord Haw Haw said. His voice dropped, became oh so sweet and kind. "And dear citizens of Belfast, you've had a taste of our Luftwaffe's

136

power. Sleep well, for tonight you shall have a respite. But we'll be back. Wait for us."

I moved the diode quickly, partly because my heart was hammering with fear and anger and partly because it was unpatriotic to listen to Haw Haw. He spouted only German lies and propaganda. It was all right if you laughed and talked back to him, as my father did sometimes, but I didn't feel up to laughing or talking back tonight.

Now I had Joe Loss and his band playing "In the Mood." It came at me in little jumps and starts, with somebody's voice talking Gaelic through it and over it. I couldn't tune it in. I'd wasted a whole pound on this worthless contraption.

Was Miss Müller still crying? I took out the earplug and heard the tiniest squeak. What was that? I sat up in bed, moved the crystal set carefully out of my way. Miss Müller's door. It couldn't be. She was going out. I held my breath.

Those were her footsteps, soft and almost silent as they whispered their way up the dorm. My mind fumbled around. We'd thought she wouldn't go tonight. I'd have to waken everyone. I'd have to wait till it was safe. I listened intently. No sound now. She'd gone. She was out of the dorm.

I grabbed my dressing gown and slippers, got my flashlight, went fast into Lizard's room, shone the light smack in her face.

"Quick! Quick! Miss Müller's spy walking after all."

I ran to Ada's room, pulling on my dressing gown as I went, and shook her shoulder. She was awake before I shook twice. I rushed into Maureen's cubie.

137

With Maureen it took a minute. It took longer. It took Ada's help. It took too long. We dragged her out of bed, Lizard carrying Maureen's flashlight with her own, Ada stuffing Mo into her dressing gown. Maureen had big pink rollers in her hair, the ones Ada said made her curls look like the city sewer pipes when she took them out.

"Give me a second," Maureen kept mumbling. "Hey, let me wake up, will you?"

"We don't have time. Get awake now," Ada said.

We all had our flashlights switched on. There was no need to be careful—Miss Müller wasn't even there. But when we came to Long Parlor I whispered, "Put them out and be quiet. We don't want to waken Greta."

"Greta's gone," Lizard said.

Her blanket lay on the floor. The black vinyl sofa was empty. Oh no.

We went single file along the corridor holding on to one another's dressing-gown cords. I was in the lead, then Lizard, then Mo, then Ada, pushing Maureen from behind. Our shadows walked with us.

Through the main hallway we went, the big shield-shaped front door with its studding of nail heads close-bolted against the night. Then under the portraits, their waxy faces coming and going as our flashlight beams slid across them. Past Old Rose's sitting room. She'd be comfortably asleep in her bedroom in back, snug under her fat eiderdown, sure that all her Alveara girls and mistresses, too, were safe and sound asleep.

Up the red-carpeted staircase, our hands following the wide banister.

"Flashlights off," I whispered at the top.

We stood, listening. Not a sound. Not a sign of Miss Müller or Greta. But they'd gotten a head start on us.

We moved in silence past the closed san door, past the dispensary and Nursie's bedroom. Here was the archway to the roof stairs.

We stopped and Maureen gave a little whimper. "We can't go up there in the dark." Her hands clutched at me. "We have to have our flashlights on or we'll break our necks."

"Shield the beams," I said.

"What if we meet Marjorie?" Maureen begged.

"We won't," Ada said. "Marjorie's dead."

I had this awful urge now to hurry. Whatever Miss Müller was doing, we had to stop her. And if Greta was there, we had to stop her from stopping Miss Müller in her own way.

My flashlight fluttered ahead of me on the cold gray steps that led into darkness. The other three round lights jumped the steps behind me. Our slippers sounded soft as leaves falling from an oak tree. The coffin room. Yes, Marjorie was dead, but still we climbed faster as we passed it.

Cold air drifted down now that we were close to the roof. What was our plan? We didn't have one. Greta had asked that, too. "Will you kill her?" No, no, not kill. I had an idea. When we found Miss Müller, three of us would hold her, the other would run down and ring Nursie's bell. Ring it and ring it and hammer on her door. Yes, that would work. That would be good. Nursie would be raging at first, but then she'd understand. Nursie was tough.

Here was the step to the roof. I turned to face the

others. "Flashlights off," I whispered, clicking off mine. "Be careful."

I stepped out onto the roof.

Light rain misted down; the sky was clotted with clouds. If there was a moon, it was behind the tower. What time was it anyway? I couldn't see the blacked-out face of the clock. Was it midnight yet? It was so dark up there without even a glow from the faraway sky. I remembered the buckets of sand and water. Behind me somebody tripped coming over the step. It was Ada. I heard her mutter, "Criminy!"

We were all out, huddling in wet misery, trying to see through the blackness.

When the voice spoke, Maureen gave a high little shriek.

"It's Greta," the voice said. "Müller's not here." A flashlight came on. Behind it I saw the shape of Greta, her long dark hair, the darker pools of her eyes.

"Douse that light, or cover it up," I told her quickly. "We're outside. There could be planes."

She cupped the light. The red glowed through her fingers, like skeleton bones. That hand held something else. The nail file, silvery red, too, and deadly.

"What do you mean she's not here?" Ada whispered. "You followed her, didn't you? This is where she's supposed to always come."

"I followed her. She came."

"You didn't push her over?" Maureen stepped back until she was behind Ada.

"She wasn't here to push," Greta said. "Follow me and I'll show you something."

140

We followed. Greta stopped at the edge of the roof and pointed down.

"This is how she gets away to do whatever she's doing," she said.

We peered into the darkness below. Greta cupped her flashlight and shone its light down. The metal fire escape hugged the ivy-covered walls and marched all the way to the gravel driveway at the bottom.

"Easy to use," Greta said in disgust.

It would be easy. The fire escape wasn't just an iron ladder but a gridlike staircase with turns and platforms at each level.

"She could be anywhere," Greta said, waving an arm. "In one of the other buildings, in the shrubbery, in Whitla Hall . . . anywhere. Alveara is locked up tight at night, but this is always open. This is her way to freedom."

We clustered together, staring down at the shadowed grounds and beyond them to the street. A trolley bus, its windows darkened, its guide rails throwing off blue sparks, glided noisily past the Alveara gates.

"Should we go down ourselves and try to find her?" I asked.

"Where would we start to look?" Greta asked.

Maureen gave a couple of little hops. "I vote we go inside." She touched her sponge rollers. "These things soak up the wet. I'll be a frizzy lizzie all day tomorrow."

"Honestly, Maureen," Ada said. "You haven't the sense God gave a muskrat."

"Miss Müller has to come up the way she went down," I said. "We'll wait."

"We could wait at the bottom of the stairs and nab her when she steps out," Lizard suggested.

Ada pushed at air with her free hand. "If she doesn't want to tell us where she's been, we'll scare it out of her."

"Great idea." Greta was turned away from me, the nail file a dull gleam in the hand that hung by her side. I pounced, grabbed, and had it.

"Hey!" she said.

"You won't be needing this," I said, and slipped it into my pocket.

"You Irish girls do not understand about the enemy," Greta said.

"Oh, yeah?" Maureen asked. "So why are we here? Do you think you're the only one who loves her country and who hates the Germans? We weren't coming up here to have a picnic with Miss Müller, you know."

"Relax, Mo," I said. "Just relax."

We hurried back down the stairs, warning each other not to fall, not to step on heels. Lizzie Mag was behind me holding my dressing-gown cord.

"Jess." There was something odd in her voice. The cord jerked as she stopped. I stopped too.

"What?"

"Look." Her voice was as pale as her face in the white light that shone up from her flashlight. She turned its beam on the coffin-room door.

You had to really look before you saw it. The heavy chain was still around the knob, but the padlock that hung from it gaped open.

"Was it like this when we came up?" I whispered. Something strange was happening to my legs; a chill shiver cold as a cockroach ran up and down my skin.

We didn't know. We hadn't looked on the way up.

"Heaven preserve us, Marjorie's out," Maureen whispered. We pressed ourselves against the wall.

Greta pushed in front of Lizard so carelessly that I said, "Watch out," and grabbed at Lizard's arm as she toppled on the step, then righted herself.

"The German is in the coffin room," Greta said. She reached across me and flung open the door.

17

THE COFFIN-ROOM DOOR was open, the inside dark as a tomb except where our flashlights probed. Not one of us had ever seen inside before. Maybe we'd expected a trestle with a coffin on it, Marjorie lying in state the way the girl vampire lay in *Dracula*. What we saw was Miss Müller standing in her black dressing gown, and beside her, her hand in his, Mr. Bolton.

We stared, stunned to silence. One wavering flashlight picked out the blue in his plaid dressing gown, shone on his glasses and round, pale face. Another showed a bunk bed, just like the ones in our dorm, neatly made up, the white sheet smooth across the blanket. There was a small table with a lamp, and two straight-backed chairs.

"Miss Müller?" Lizzie Mag whispered.

Miss Müller moved quietly to the table and switched on the lamp. It had a pink shade. The table was an old treadle sewing machine with the top closed. There were things scattered on it: a blue jar with the lid off, a candle in an old-fashioned holder, two flashlights, and a little glass bottle that held a single purple rhododendron.

"We should have made our escape while you were on the roof," Miss Müller said. Her voice had no life in it.

"John thought you would come down very quickly and you'd see us."

John was Mr. Bolton. J. P. Bolton, B.A., M.A., my Latin teacher. Sweet, ordinary Mr. Bolton who'd shielded Miss Müller from the hissing in the dining room, who'd walked with her from assembly.

"We decided that going up to the roof was some sort of dare," he said. "Was it?"

"No. We were following Miss Müller."

"Oh." He sounded puzzled.

Miss Müller spoke away from Mr. Bolton, away from us. "I'm sorry that I got you into this, John. I wasn't worth it."

Now I could see the greasy marks high on the shoulders of her dressing gown. She'd put ointment on the sore places where the brush had scrubbed, or maybe he'd smoothed the cream on for her.

"Don't be sorry . . . please don't be sorry. You are worth the world," he said.

She stood still, not looking at him or us, rigid, like some beautiful statue. As lifeless as a vampire in a coffin, I thought.

Mr. Bolton ran a hand over his thinning hair and sighed. "She didn't do anything, you know. She did nothing to make you treat her the way you did."

I started to say, "We didn't do anything. It wasn't *us* put the egg on the door." But I stopped. Of course we'd done things. We'd turned against her.

"You mean she wasn't a spy?" Maureen asked.

"I was half German and that was enough," Miss Müller said to Mr. Bolton.

145

Ada slitted her eyes. "Your father was a Nazi. We know that."

"Yes," Miss Müller said, "he was. I loved him, and I was ashamed of him. Now I'm ashamed that I was ashamed. It's wrong to feel that way when you love. Love should be stronger." Her voice was monotonous, no note of sadness in it or sorrow.

Greta pushed past us. With a rush of her hand she swept the rhododendron to the floor. Water splashed across the bunk. "You . . . you Germans," she said. "You have no right to be in the company of decent people. No right." Her voice shook and she turned and stumbled out of the coffin room. Thank goodness I'd taken the nail file away from her. The rest of us shuffled uneasily.

Mr. Bolton touched Miss Müller's cheek. "She doesn't mean it, Daphne. She's just a little girl who has been through too many horrors. She wants to hurt back, and you are all she has to hurt."

"And what have I been through?" Miss Müller wailed. "What have I been through?" She ran to him and he gathered her into his arms and she leaned against him as if we weren't even there.

"Come on," I muttered, and we pushed one another out the door and down the steps, hurrying to get away from something that wasn't our world, that wasn't even in our understanding.

We huddled in the bathroom, unsure, talking in whispers.

"What have we done?" Lizard moaned. "What have we done?"

"He was her friend," I mumbled. "He comforted her."

146

Maureen sighed. "He loves her. Anyone can see. It was a romantic tryst, and even though he's not handsome, he almost is."

"How did he get up to the coffin room all those times, though?" Ada asked. "You'd think Nursie or someone would have seen or heard him." Then she nodded, answering herself. "He climbed the fire escape, of course, straight as a homing pigeon."

Maureen sighed again. "A brief encounter," she said.

"I wonder why they didn't get married." I was thinking out loud.

"Teachers here can't be married to each other, remember?" Ada said. "They both would have been fired."

"They'll be fired now," I said, and added, "unless we don't tell."

Lizard had her hand over her heart. "Oh, let's not. Let's promise to never ever tell." Tears were in the corners of her eyes.

"Greta will tell," Ada said. We looked at each other, knowing truth when we heard it.

"Should we go to her cubie right now and beg . . ." I began.

"You could give her the moon and she'd still tell," Ada said. "Unless . . ."

"Unless?" Lizard moved closer.

"Unless you can bring back her father," Ada said. "That's the holy only of it. And that's not going to happen. Even Winston Churchill himself couldn't arrange that."

Greta told.

Miss Müller was asked to leave. Two days later she

147

was gone. As Greta said: "There are more ways of killing a cockroach than swinging it by its tail."

"What does *that* mean?" Maureen asked.

"It means Miss Müller might as well be dead as out of work now, here in Belfast," I explained.

Greta stuck her hands in her blazer pockets. "I thought we were going to stick together against the dictator," she said. "Wasn't that the way it was supposed to be?"

"She wasn't a dictator," I said. "She was just a person. And I hope you're happy now, Greta Ludowski."

Greta gave me one of her deep, dark, forever looks. "I'm not expecting to be happy," she said.

The night before Miss Müller left, I heard her go up to the bathroom and I followed her and waited. "I'm sorry," I said miserably. "We're all sorry."

"Es macht nichts," she said, and shrugged. There were hollows in her cheeks, and her eyes looked at me as if she'd never seen me before. Es macht nichts. It doesn't matter.

Mr. Bolton was not fired.

"It's just like what happened to Pearl Carson and the mighty Michael Moran," Ada said. "Boys will be boys and the woman's a slut."

But there was a difference. Mr. Bolton resigned and we heard he joined the army. We missed him too. We talked about the time he said this strange grace for about a month: "Aut id devorabis amabisque, aut cras prandebis." It was ages before anyone figured out that it meant "Either you'll eat it and like it, or you'll have it for breakfast tomorrow." It had sounded so devout when he said it. We'd liked him so much for doing things like that.

A week after the first air raid we had another ferocious

148

one. The city was almost leveled. Two hundred pounds of high-explosive bombs were dropped and seven hundred people were killed. This time we didn't have Miss Müller to blame. A month later the Luftwaffe hit Belfast again and dropped ninety-six thousand incendiary bombs. By now we had stopped thinking that going to the shelter in the basement was fun.

"Dear people of Belfast, your city is burning," Lord Haw Haw said smugly. It was burning from end to end, from the Cavehill to Castlereagh. From the Falls to Sydenham. Our school was untouched, though, so I stayed on.

Ada's parents took her and Jack home out of danger. She's a day girl at Dungannon High now and she hates it. She says the girls are all sticks. She has already sent us tuck boxes, Marmite, and anything else she can scrounge. We've got Dolly McConnell and her teeth wires in Ada's cubie. Dolly's okay. She says she wishes we'd stop calling it Ada's room. It's her room now, but we can't seem to get that into our heads.

Pat Crow has been sent to boarding school outside Toronto, Canada. That seems the other end of the world. We're glad Ada's at least closer.

Maureen has finished her balaclava and dispatched it. She's waiting for a letter from the lucky soldier who got her work of art, and letting her eyebrows grow out. It's the new Joan Crawford look.

Ian McManus and I write letters, and we have a special hidden postbox under one of the pillar stubs by the missing front gates. I send his on to Ada after I've read them. They're safer away from the maids. I have a problem, though. Ian wants me to meet him behind the gym, where I'd have to kiss him instead of his letters.

Kissing once by accident was all right, but I'm not sure I'm ready to do it on purpose.

I think a lot about a lot of things. About Bryan. Aunt Clara and Uncle Eammon had a letter from him and they are ecstatic. Uncle Eammon is keeping Bryan's Norton 350 tuned up and at the ready so the two of us can go zooming up the Sperrin Mountains to Glenshane Pass as soon as the war's over and Bryan can come home.

I think about the war and I believe them when they tell us we're winning it. A lot of people say the Americans will be coming to fight with us. We're hoping we'll see some handsome GIs; that's what the Americans call their soldiers.

I think a lot about Miss Müller and the things she said that night in the coffin room, the night we found her and Mr. Bolton. I can't forget what she said. I remember it all, word for word. "I loved him, and I was ashamed of him. Now I'm ashamed that I was ashamed. It's wrong to feel that way when you love."

Soon it will be the long summer holidays and Lizzie Mag will be left alone at Alveara except for some of the teachers and Old Rose and Boots.

One night she and I are in her cubie. Lizzie Mag is standing in front of her mirror putting in her rows of pin curls. Farther up the dorm Maureen is warbling "God Save the King," but she has American words that none of the rest of us know. They're on a song sheet she got in Woolworth's:

My country, 'tis of thee,
Sweet land of liberty . . .

Maureen's *really* hoping!

I watch Lizzie Mag roll a curl into a little flat circle, put a clip across it. "Lizard." I try to keep my voice steady. "Will you come home with me for the summer holidays? We can go bike riding and swim in the Moyola, and . . ."

In the mirror I see her eyes open wide. "But what about your daddy? Isn't he too sick . . . ?"

I interrupt while my courage is still with me. "My father isn't sick in *that* way." My tongue seems to be swelling inside my mouth, making it hard to speak. "He drinks," I say. "He's drunk most of the time."

"Oh, Jess." Lizzie Mag's hugging me. Her pin-curl clips dig into me, but I don't care. The words are out. The dread words. I've always thought saying them would be a betrayal of my father. Saying them, having my friends know, would make me die of shame. But it isn't like that. I feel I'm in an open meadow, filled with sunshine, running free under a blue sky. "He can't seem to stop," I say, and I try to smile. "Still, where there's life there's hope, and I love him so much. I love him anyway."

"I know you do," Lizzie Mag says shakily. We stand a little away from each other. "I love my father so much, too. I love *him* 'anyway.' "

I think she's going to say more about that "anyway," but she doesn't.

Over the summer, lying in my bedroom at home, or sitting on the bank of the Moyola, maybe Lizzie Mag will tell me. Then maybe we can talk about the hurtful things in our lives and the good things, and help each other.

"Lights out, girls," Miss Hardcastle calls from the top of the dorm. She's our mistress now in Snow White. She doesn't come into our cubies one by one to say good night the way Miss Müller did. Instead she stands by the light switch and waits impatiently, then plunges us into darkness.

Sometimes I lie there listening to the trams clattering up the Lisburn Road, to the quad clock striking, to Maureen's endless snores. I listen for the heart-stopping wail of the air-raid sirens.

Every night I think of Miss Müller and Mr. Bolton. I imagine them married and happy, though I don't know if that will ever happen. Miss Müller is the way she was when I first knew her. She's light and laughing again, a beautiful daffodil. In my imaginings she forgives us and understands that we never hated her, that she was just the only German at Alveara.

Sometimes in the night I think I smell apricots.

If you liked
SPYING ON MISS MÜLLER,
you'll love this other novel by Eve Bunting!

A SUDDEN SILENCE

Jesse Harmon remembers the car speeding toward his brother Bry and him in the night. He knows he screamed to his brother to get out of the way. But his brother was deaf and couldn't hear Jesse shout, and the driver killed Bry and sped away.

Filled with grief and guilt, Jesse joins Bry's girlfriend, Chloe, in a search to find the hit-and-run driver. But to add to Jesse's guilt, he begins to fall in love with Chloe.

A SUDDEN SILENCE
by Eve Bunting

Published by Fawcett Books.
Available in your local bookstore.

EVE BUNTING

Great stories . . . characters who feel like friends.